# 44

# Book Four

Jools Sinclair

## Praise for *44*...

# 44

# Book Four

## Jools Sinclair

You Come Too Publishing

*44 Book Four*

Published by You Come Too Publishing, Bend, Oregon.

Printed in the United States of America

First edition, 2012

ISBN-13: 978-1478392040
ISBN-10: 1478392045

*For Buddy...*

# Chapter 1

The wind pushed through the trees as I stood in the darkness of my bedroom watching the black branches sway back and forth, touching the moon and the stars and the clouds that raced across the sky, disappearing in the distance.

"I'm okay," I whispered, trying to slow my pounding heart. "I'm home."

A train howled in the distance, filling the night with loneliness. I opened the window and a gust of icy wind ate at my face, drying the sweat that was dripping down my forehead.

I inhaled slowly. Again and again and again. Sucking down the cold air and trying to shake off the dread that flooded through my body.

I glanced back at the glow of the numbers on the alarm clock.

*2:23*

It had just been a dream, the nightmare that was haunting me, the one that I brought back from the island where I had been held prisoner. The dreams were all the same. I was in water, swimming hard and fast away from the house and out into the large, black swells of the Pacific. I was tired, my strength leaking away with each stroke. Then I couldn't go any farther, couldn't force my arms and legs to move and I started sinking down into the watery darkness, staring up at the bright sunlight above me while I held my breath.

"Take a breath, Abby," he said, his voice soft and sweet like a daffodil opening in the warm spring sun. "Die, and then I will bring you back."

He floated above me through the waves of water and light, those intense cat eyes, dancing with excitement.

I shuddered and rubbed my arms as I remembered the dream, so vivid and clear and dark. I pushed my hair back behind my ears as I moved over toward my bed and sat down. I touched the clock on my nightstand. Touched my pillow. My blankets. I looked over at the desk and stared at my computer, a silver necklace wrapped around a picture frame.

These were all my things. I was in my own room.

I was home.

I put on my robe and wandered back over to the window and looked out at the yard lit up under a large, bright moon.

"Just a dream," I said again. "I'm home."


*2:45*

A thin moonbeam stretched across the floor. I sat at my desk looking at the small stuffed panda I won at a fair when I was little, the Messi poster hanging on the wall, the Barcelona soccer scarf wrapped around my bedpost. On my bulletin board was the Kathleen Edwards ticket from the concert I went to a few years ago, pinned up next to my high school diploma.

During the day, I walked by all these things, not noticing them, not even thinking about them. In the daylight, they gathered dust. But now, in the dark hours before dawn, I realized how much they meant.

### 3:13

The noise startled me.

I went over and closed the window quickly, pushing down the lock. I looked out, searching for some movement as I tried to steady my breathing.

It could have been a lot of things. The deer that sometimes ate from the neighbor's bird feeder, the cat two houses over that prowled around in the early morning hours, the wind blowing through the chimes. I stayed there, watching the night, until all the silhouettes made sense.

I stayed there at the window for a while. A long while, until I was sure nothing was there.

### 3:50

I left the light off in the bathroom, splashed cold water on my face and caught my reflection and gasped.

In the faint light, I looked like a ghost.

I stared back at the dead girl in the mirror.

### 5:44

I pulled the thick, white comforter around me. It made me feel safe as I listened to the groans and creaks of the house against the wind, vigilant for anything that didn't belong.

But there was nothing. I yawned, resting my head on the pillow, and waited.

The bittersweet light of dawn filtered through the curtains, taking me down through the layers of dreams, finally ushering me back into the illusive world of sleep.

# Chapter 2

Out of the corner of my eye, I saw the Subaru pull up into the parking lot and squeeze into the last empty space.

"Abby Craig!" David yelled from behind the espresso machine, startling me. "Yo sista's in da house."

Kate had gotten in the habit of stopping in at Back Street Coffee a few times during the week when I was working. I knew she was checking up on me because she liked Thump Coffee better. But I didn't mind and I usually tried to take my breaks with her.

I finished taking the order from the woman with dark hair and thin lips and handed back her change. The next customer, a regular who always had tired eyes and a loosened tie, wanted a large black coffee so I poured it myself and handed it to him.

"Thanks," he said, throwing a dollar bill in the tip jar.

A loud eruption of laughter shot through the window. I looked over at the small group huddled together outside, standing in a circle. They were young and looked like they had come back from the mountain, dressed in parkas and beanies pulled tight down around their long hair that stuck out in strands. Even though it was April, it was still pretty cold. Snow was in the forecast for the city. But the sun was strong and people liked being outside around the metal tables and chairs while they soaked in the icy rays.

Kate came through the door and headed straight for the last empty table in the back. Her hair bounced a little as she waved at me. She was wearing her new Frye boots and they pounded on the wood floors as she walked through the crowd. I looked over at David, who had been staring at her feet.

"Cowgirl in the house," he said as he pulled a shot of espresso.

He walked away from the counter and moved quickly in her direction. Back Street Coffee didn't have waiters but ever since she had used a few of David's quotes in a story she had written about the Tower Theatre, Kate was his new best friend.

Mo, short for Maureen, sighed loudly from behind a thick band of steam rising up toward the ceiling and moved over to the machine that David had abandoned. I helped the large guy wearing a Red Sox baseball cap and called out the order. Mo didn't look up or acknowledge what I had said, like always, but I watched her reach for the non-fat milk and knew that she had heard me.

"It'll be just a moment," I told him and he moved down and waited in front of Mo, staring at her tattoos.

Kate set her things down and wandered back up and said hello while David walked over to the bar to start her drink.

"Hey," I said. "How's it going?"

"Good," she said, her eyes scanning the large glass case filled with pastries. "You?"

"Good, too."

"And I'll take one of those," she said, pointing to a blueberry scone. Then she lowered her voice to just above a whisper. "Your friend over there is sure, well, friendly."

"I think you mean *our* friend," I said. "So how long do you have today?"

"Not too long," she said, running her fingers through her hair. "I've got to cover a press conference at two. But can you take a break? I need to talk to you."

"Yeah. I'll let Mike know."

David handed Kate her drink in a large, white ceramic mug. She smiled after she looked at it and I knew that he had put a chocolate powder heart on top of the white foam. He did that for his special customers.

"I'll be over there working," she said. I handed her the scone and she walked away.

Lately when Kate said she needed to talk to me, it just meant one thing. The investigation. But I didn't really want to talk about it, not here at work anyway and not on my break. But she never understood that. Whenever she heard something, she always wanted to tell me immediately. She was thinking I was like her, that I also had that same anger burning deep inside and that I would want to know about any new developments right away. She was on the phone regularly with the special agent in charge of my case, checking for updates even though they said they would call when they had anything new to report.

She thought it would bring me comfort. That the case was moving along. That progress was being made.

But mostly I didn't care. I mean, sure, I wanted those people to pay for what they did to me. It was wrong. I knew it wasn't altogether realistic, but I wanted to get on with my life. And as impossible as it was, I wanted to forget about Nathaniel Mortimer and his band of ghouls.

It had been just over five months since I was rescued from a private island in the Puget Sound, since Kate and Dr. Mortimer and a small group of security agents found me locked away in a house.

Charges had been pressed against the four members of Nathaniel's crew who had been captured, including Simon. The FBI didn't come out and say as much, but Kate suspected that Simon ended up confessing and cut a deal with the authorities, agreeing to testify against the others. But everything was moving slowly and we were told that the trial was still several months away.

Fortunately, the police and the Bureau had seen fit to keep my name out of their press releases and statements. So when the story hit the newspapers and went viral, no one knew that I was involved. And it was a big story. Pretty much everything except for my identity had come out. It went national, all the major newspapers and news shows talking about how a girl had been kidnapped by a group of crazy doctors who thought they had found an antidote for death.

About how two of the scientists had escaped.

And about how one man had killed his insane brother.

It was a circus and I was lucky not to be a part of it. But once I testified, all that would change. My identity would no longer be protected. My days were numbered. My life as a Frankenstein experiment would soon be exposed. It was coming, possibly as soon as winter.

Kate said she didn't have any mixed feelings having to sit on such a huge story. But I told her that as long as other people were going to eventually be telling the story and attaching my name to it, she should too.

"We'll deal with that when it happens," she said.

"You might want to start writing it now," I said. "It could be, what do you call that? Oh, yeah, first person. And be a series. I know you'd do a great job. And you'd get all the facts right."

"Yeah, it's got Pulitzer written all over it," she had said sarcastically.

"I'm serious," I said.

But for now, I took refuge in the anonymity. For now, I had spring and summer. Maybe even fall.

For now, I could slip back into my life. Play soccer, work at the coffee house, hang out with Ty. Be a river guide in the summer. Go to concerts.

A few more people wandered in from outside and I quickly walked over to David.

"I'm going to take a break," I told him.

"Sure you are," he said, taking over the register.

"Thanks."

I liked working with David and was always happy when I saw his name on the schedule next to mine.

I walked toward the back room, meeting Mo's eyes for a second as she brewed a new pot of the house blend. She didn't say anything, as usual. It didn't matter how cold it was, she always wore the same kind of tank top under her apron, which exposed her tattoo-covered arms. And no matter how hard I tried, I always stared at the dark ink that shot up toward her shoulders, stopping myself only after I saw the large cross or the guitar.

I found Mike in the back, behind the shelves.

"I'm gonna take my break now, if that's okay," I said.

I tried to talk softly, so I wouldn't startle him because it was always easy to scare people in the back room. It was dark and the strong aromas and all those beans seemed to muffle the noise so you never knew if somebody was coming.

"Yeah, sure," he said, jumping awkwardly. "Of course. It must be time. I'll come up front and help cover the counter."

Mike was short and thin, with light hair and a small goatee that he often stroked when he seemed to be thinking about something. His energy was calm and he was soft spoken, no matter how loud it got.

"How's it been out there?" he asked, adjusting his silver-rimmed glasses. I heard Diana Krall playing on the stereo and knew David must have put the music on for Kate.

"Busy," I said. "As usual."

"Good," he said, dropping a dark apron over his head. "That's how we like it."

I was glad he wanted me to return to work after I got back to Bend. I never told him the specifics of what had really happened, but when I got home, I emailed him, telling him that a family emergency had forced me to leave town suddenly. I was surprised at his reaction. The next week I was back on the schedule like nothing had ever happened.

When we walked out, a long line stretched all the way to the door. I hesitated.

"We got it," Mike said. "Enjoy your break, Abby."

Back Street Coffee had become the new hot spot in Bend. When I had started working, mostly it was full of snowboarders and skiers coming home after their runs. It was the kind of place Jesse and I would have come to after a good morning on the mountain. But in the last few months, word had spread how amazing the coffee was, and now all sorts of people came in. Business people, court people, cyclists, workers from downtown. Business was so good that Mike told us that they were thinking of opening another store.

I poured a small cup of freshly brewed coffee, adding in lots of cream, and then headed over toward Kate.

# Chapter 3

"We could go outside if you want," Kate asked, closing her laptop and pushing it to the far corner of the table.

"This is fine," I said. "Besides, it's crowded out there, too. And cold."

I couldn't wait until summer, when the sun had warmth to it and I could get back to T-shirts and shorts. Sometimes the cold weather lasted too long. I always felt that way in the spring. It took forever to transition into warm days.

"It's always so busy in this place," she said, staring at the group of six women at the table next to us. They worked at the bank. "I feel lucky to be able to just find an empty seat."

"Oh, you'll never have a problem with that as long as David is around," I said. "He'll kick someone out for you."

She smiled and pulled up her hair, tying it in a loose knot behind her head.

She drained her cup and squinted at the sun that was now streaming in through the window. I brought down the blinds a little and sat down again, leaning back in the wobbly plastic chair, studying her as she looked around. Her eyes were large and jittery, like she hadn't been sleeping much either.

"Any plans this weekend?" I asked, stirring my coffee and then taking a sip. It was still too hot to drink.

"Painting," she said.

It began right after my rescue. Kate started fixing up the house. At first, I thought it wasn't such a big deal, but over the months it had become an obsession. Instead of spending long nights at the newspaper like she used to, she now stayed home painting. She became a Home Depot and Lowes junkie, roaming the aisles in her free time, comparing styles and prices on new appliances and bathroom tiles and crown molding. She had already painted almost every room in the house, and had me help her pick out new granite countertops for the kitchen. She had bought new living room furniture as well, including two new leather sofas with studs down the side seams, a coffee table that looked like an old treasure chest, and lamps made out of juniper branches.

We had a small savings account our mom left us when she died. Personally, I could think of lots of other things I would have used the money for. But it seemed important to Kate in a way I didn't fully understand.

Our little house had never looked so good.

She leaned back in her chair and stared off, deep in thought. She smiled finally, looking at her scone.

I hesitated and then went for it.

"So what did you want to talk about?"

"Oh, yeah," she said. "I know you said I should choose the paint color for your room, but I'm torn between two. Do you have a preference?"

She pulled out two small paint chips and handed them to me.

I smiled, relieved as I looked them over.

When I drowned in that mountain lake almost four years ago, I was brought back to life but some things were different. Since the accident I see people's energy circulating around them and can read how they are feeling. I see ghosts occasionally. And although I haven't had one in a while, sometimes I have visions.

The other big change is that I'm color blind and live in a world of blacks, whites, and grays.

I handed Kate the darker shade.

"This one," I said.

"Good," she said. "Want a bite?"

"No, thanks."

I was trying to cut down on my pastry intake, which had skyrocketed since I began working here. I felt sluggish when I practiced or went for runs. Soccer season was still a few months away, but it was time to get ready.

I watched three cyclists walk in and get in line. They were all wearing those tight-fitting racing outfits with numbers and geometric designs all over. Maybe there was an event in town, but even with the mild winter, it still seemed too early for bike races.

"So, what are you and Ty up to this weekend?" Kate asked.

"Probably catch a movie," I said.

Kate smiled as I yawned.

"He's really serious about you. I mean he's still hanging around even after you made him watch *Water for Elephants* over at the house the other night."

"Yeah, that was a real dog," I said. "I'm letting him pick the next one."

"Hey, how did you sleep last night?"

I shrugged, and as if on cue, yawned again.

"Same."

I didn't like to talk too much about my nights. I didn't want her to worry and I especially didn't want her to start in again about me going back to see my old psychiatrist,

Dr. Krowe. I knew she heard me sometimes when I was up, walking around the house, waiting for my fear to settle down and dissipate so I could catch at least a few hours of sleep. No matter how quiet I tried to be, the house creaked under my feet at those hours. Plus, Kate was a light sleeper.

She stared at me.

"I'm fine," I said. "Really. It's getting better, I think."

"Bull," she said. "Look, Abby, I know you don't want to take sleeping pills, and I get that. But if you don't start getting some regular sleep soon, your system is going to break down. You are going to break down. You aren't looking that great. You can't go on like this."

She said she did, but she didn't get it. I had had a bad reaction to the drugs Nathaniel gave me when he kidnapped me. The pain was so horrible I thought I would die. But it was nothing compared to the feelings of helplessness, loss of control, and being held prisoner. In my head that's what sleeping pills meant and it would be a cold day in hell before I took them.

"I know all that," I said anyway. "A few more weeks. If it doesn't get better, I'll go see him, get the pills and everything. Promise."

Kate sighed and stretched.

"All right," she said. "A few more weeks, but that's it. It's normal, you know. You've been through a traumatic event. They treat these conditions successfully. I've been doing research on it."

I held back a sigh of my own.

"I'm going to send you some links. Just read about it, okay?"

"Yeah," I said.

I wasn't sure why, but seeing Dr. Krowe felt like going backwards. I agreed with what Kate was saying, that I needed to start having normal sleep again. But seeing him again and discussing all the things that had happened didn't feel right. Kate wasn't going to stop though and it made me glad that I hadn't told her about all the nightmares.

She stood up.

"I gotta get going," she said. "What time will you be home?"

"I'm practicing after work so not until after seven."

"Riverbend Park?" she asked.

I nodded.

"Is Ty meeting you?"

"No, Kate. But I'll be okay. Lots of people are always there and the sun stays out late these days."

"Okay," she said. "Don't forget to call when you're on your way home."

"I won't."

It still took some getting used to, having to check in with Kate all the time. But after what had happened with Jack Martin in the parking lot, I always made sure to call her and let her know where I was, especially if I was by myself.

"I won't forget," I repeated.

She packed up her computer and notebook and shoved them into her bag.

She waved goodbye and walked through the crowd and out the door.

# Chapter 4

A misty rain fell from a blinding, white sky as I ran up to the far end of the grass and threw down my water bottle. I didn't mind getting wet. It felt good being outside, and at least it wasn't snowing.

I zipped up the Barcelona jacket Ty had gotten me for Christmas and then scrolled to the new playlist I had put together the night before. I put my keys deep in my pocket before starting, the soccer ball sluggish at my feet in the wet grass.

Even with the cold rain there were a lot of people at the park. A few were walking their dogs. A group of young women ran past me, their voices and breathing loud, mixing in with the beat of my music. A mom pushed a baby stroller on the cement path that skirted the grass.

I hit the timer on my watch and started running, thinking about soccer. Jack Martin suddenly popped into my mind.

It wasn't like I thought Jack would come back for me. I knew that with Nathaniel dead, so was the research. And really, Jack had been nothing more than a glorified assistant, a henchman. The FBI investigators told us that while he was still a wanted fugitive, they doubted that he would ever return for me. It would have been too much of a risk and they suspected he was probably living under another alias in another country.

I didn't lose any sleep over him. What made me uncomfortable was that just about everyone who played soccer through Parks and Rec knew Jack. Or they thought they knew him. And when we both went missing following an indoor soccer game last November, rumors had started.

According to one story, Jack and I had eloped. A few people joked about wedding presents and asked where we had registered. Even though the whole idea made me sick, I tried to play along, not wanting to appear too defensive or that I had something to hide. That I knew something.

But at some point the jokes stopped and some of his friends began to worry that something had happened to him. They filed a missing person report, but the police told them that the authorities were already looking for him, that "Jack Martin" was a person of interest in an FBI investigation.

There had to be a mistake, his friends said. He wasn't the kind of person to be involved in something like that, whatever that *something* was. I couldn't help thinking about all those crime shows I used to watch late at night. There were always those friends and neighbors of killers saying that the murderer was "such a nice guy."

I almost laughed thinking I would have felt the same way about him before. Before he kidnapped me, I had thought Jack was a nice guy too. That's how he was able to kidnap me. Even though I had noticed his strange energy on more than one occasion, I was sure he was a friend. The whole experience had left me feeling stupid and angry at myself. But I was determined to learn from it and move on.

I figured it might be a little awkward at first, but that after a few games people would forget about Jack. Until then, I would just have to focus on keeping my lunch down whenever his name came up.

I kicked the ball too far ahead and it rolled over by the river, stopping just short of the sloped embankment. I walked down to the water, staring out at the Deschutes gliding by peacefully as I caught my breath.

"Nice jacket," I heard from behind.

I lost my balance for a moment as I turned, following the voice. It belonged to a man, about 30, wearing an Athletic Bilbao jersey, drinking water from a plastic bottle.

"Thanks," I said, thinking how he was probably the only person in Bend, maybe even the entire United States, with that shirt. "You too."

But I had let my guard down. I hadn't seen the stranger, who was standing only a few feet away from me. I looked around and was surprised that no one else was nearby, just the two of us by the river. I felt for my keys in my pocket, for the Mace that was clipped onto them. I felt a little better as I touched the cylinder.

"Well, see ya," he said before running off. "*Agur*."

I should have been more aware of who was around me.

I walked in the opposite direction, trying to calm down.

"Relax," I told myself. I watched as he ran far off into the distance, only a small speck now, taking the path that led toward the Old Mill stores. I started dribbling again.

I went for another half an hour, in the end leaving behind the jittery feeling. Most of the time, I was good about paying attention to my surroundings. But obviously, sometimes I wasn't.

On my last lap around the park, I looked for Jesse. I hadn't seen him for a while and was expecting him to show up soon. We usually met in the park after a run, or down by the river. But not too often. Only a couple times really since we'd gone over to his dad's motorcycle shop and had a sit down.

It had been a good meeting. Jesse said he wasn't sure if his dad had believed it, that Jesse was actually there as a ghost, but even though Mr. Stone had been quiet afterwards, I could tell by his energy that something in him had changed. He wasn't as sad. I had seen him once since our meeting, and he greeted me with open, hopeful eyes and a large smile. He believed, I could tell. And after I handed him a box full of freshly baked chocolate chip cookies, he gave me a hug and thanked me. And I knew it wasn't for the cookies.

I never called out to Jesse anymore. In the months since I had been kidnapped, I realized that he needed to move on. And it was important that he knew that I could live without him. I didn't want to, and it ached when I thought that there might be a day in the near future when I didn't see him walking along the river toward me. But I was trying really hard to show him that I could do it. That I could make it on my own.

Still, it was hard to think that way. And sometimes, usually after we got to talking about basketball or soccer or the people I worked with at the coffee house, I would forget. I would forget that Jesse was a ghost, and didn't belong in this world anymore. And then, just for a minute or two, my heart would break all over again.

There was so much of Jesse's world that I didn't understand and I always got the feeling that he didn't either. He would walk with the others, the ghosts and the dead, but he didn't talk much about it. And when I asked, he said that he didn't know enough to say anything for sure.

And he told me that he would hang around for a little while longer to make sure I stayed safe. He promised he wouldn't just disappear one day.

I ran to the Jeep as the rain turned to hail.

I called Kate to tell her I was on my way home, hoping she had made dinner.

# Chapter 5

The coffee house was packed as I walked through the door on Wednesday afternoon. The three o'clock through closing shift was my favorite, even though it didn't go by as fast as the morning hours. After dinner, things got pretty quiet. But the energy in the place shifted as well. The customers were more relaxed and friendlier. And in the last hour, hardly anybody came. I was never sure why Mike wanted to stay open until nine, especially on week nights, but he seemed to think it was worth it.

After saying hello, I walked to the back and checked the schedule and saw that I was closing with Mo. We would be together, just us, for two long hours. I cringed. It wasn't that I didn't like her, it's just that I never knew what to say to her. She was even quieter than I was and when it was just the two of us working together, there were a lot of strange long silences throughout the evening. I didn't take it personally. Mo barely talked to anyone.

"What's up, Abby?" Mike said. Both David and Mo were behind the espresso bar.

"Hey," I said, taking over the register.

There were only a few people in line and I took their orders.

"Super fun times," David said to me and then told me he was taking his break.

The first few hours flew by and then the place emptied out and quieted down. Mike went home. He told us that he was forcing himself to leave and have dinner with his wife and kids at least three times a week. Mo nodded a goodbye to him without eye contact.

It seemed we were destined to have a quiet night. David went in the back to work on inventory and Mo put in the new Chilblains CD. Mike wanted to start promoting some of the local indie bands that played in the clubs on the weekends and gave us a stack of music to go through. He told us to categorize them according to the best times of day to play them. There were various genres. The alternative music could be for the afternoon and evening. And the string quartet would be perfect for the lunch hour.

David had told me that Mo played in one of the bands in the stack of CDs, and I was looking forward to hearing what she had going on besides, of course, a winning personality.

"It's harsh, harsh music," he whispered, when I had asked about her band.

Mo had been working at Back Street for three years and David was sure that she was some sort of relative of Mike's. Mo wasn't that much older than me, but she seemed like it. David said he sometimes saw her at the clubs on the weekends.

She turned up the music louder than usual, the bass pumping steadily through my body. The guitar riffs reminded me of the grunge sound of the 90s. It was pretty good stuff, and I made a note to myself to borrow the CD and add some of the songs to my running playlist.

Two men came in and I dialed down the volume. I took their orders and when their drinks were ready, they headed for opposite corners and sat at small tables.

"Going on my break," Mo said, her eyebrow rings glinting in the light. The place was empty now and I was wiping down tables, killing some time.

"Okay," I said.

I watched her for a moment as she walked outside and pulled a cigarette from her pocket, lit it and sat down on the curb. Soon she was engulfed in white smoke.

I went over to the espresso machine and dumped out the grounds into the bags that we gave out for free to gardeners, and washed out some canisters. David came back up to the front and turned down the music even lower.

"This band sucks," he said. "Hey, how's it going out here?"

"Good," I said. "You off soon?"

"If soon means right now then, yes," he said, smirking. "Scary, huh? Being left alone with Mo."

He laughed. He was just having fun. Out of everybody, David was probably Mo's favorite. He knew that I was a little intimidated by her.

"Must be awfully quiet in here with the two of you. Sorry to miss out on all the fun. Just remember. Her bark is worse than her bite. Actually, she doesn't even have a bite. Really. She's very cool. Just low energy, that's all."

I shrugged.

"So how's that beautiful boyfriend of yours?" he asked as he grabbed a towel and wiped down the counter.

I gave him a look and held it for a minute before rolling my eyes. I didn't exactly like that term, and he used it often. I wasn't even sure if Ty was exactly my boyfriend. We were friends, did things together. Kissed sometimes. I had strong feelings for him. But I told him I needed to go slow, really slow. He said he completely understood and that he wanted to give me room to recover from everything. That's what we were doing for now. So I wasn't sure if that really qualified as being a couple.

But I wasn't going to go into all that with David.

"Ty's good," I said. "How's your beautiful boyfriend?"

He laughed and leaned up against the wall.

"Wow, look at you," he said, shaking his head. "It only took five months for you to warm up to me, but here we are. Abby Craig, I never gave up hope."

David always called everyone by their first and last names, like we were all stuck in a Stephen King story. I thought it was odd the way he did that, until I found out he was actually from Maine, just like King and most of the characters in his books and movies. I guess that was just how they talked back there.

"Come on, now," I said, smiling. "I warmed up to you at least a week ago."

He laughed again.

"And by the way," David said. "Eduardo DaCosta is just fine. You should come out with us sometime. We're going to the clubs on Friday night."

David was a big partier and was always coming in looking like what the cat dragged in on Monday mornings, with lots of stories about his crazy weekends. He also had a hard time remembering that I wasn't 21 yet and couldn't get into the bars.

He looked at me, his light eyes wide, waiting for an answer.

"Can't," I said. "Not until the end of June anyway."

"Oh, yeah, I'm always forgetting that," he said. "You just don't seem 20 years old, Abby Craig. You're much older and wiser. An old spirit or something."

I nodded. It made me kind of sad, David saying that.

"Well, June's not so far away," he said. "We'll paint the town red on your birthday weekend."

"Okay," I said.

At least I had a few months to figure a way to get out of it.

"So I'm gonna go clock out," he said. "You can always call me if you can't take Mo anymo'. I'll talk you through the rest of your shift."

I laughed.

"We'll be fine. We've done it before, you know."

"Yeah, I know. I remember. That's why I'm saying it. I got your back."

I threw a towel at his head, but he ducked out of the way before it hit his face.

Mo and I said almost nothing to each other after David left, even though we were working side by side. The music had gotten louder again.

"Maybe we could close early tonight," she said as I stood by the window, watching the steady rain fall. Most of the light had left the sky.

"Sure, if you think," I said. I was sure Mike would be fine with it. He did that sometimes too if things got slow.

I yawned, stared over at her for a minute as I collected some packages of Guatemalan coffee to put out on the shelf. She had a small diamond stud in her nose. Her hair was different shades, shoulder length with lots of product so it could stand up in parts.

I tried to think of something to say or something to ask Mo, but it was hopeless. I didn't want to come across like those nervous customers who felt compelled to make small talk with her. I just let the silence sit and grabbed the broom and started sweeping as I heard the door bells chime and saw two women come in.

"Looks like you two are having a good time," one of them said. Mo didn't answer, but cut the music as I walked over to the cash register.

Most of the customers who came in were either attract-ed to Mo or scared of her. She never smiled or said much, but her piercings and tattoos earned her a certain amount of respect. Even the bank ladies and men in suits who came in at the lunch hour would be friendly, even if they looked at her with fear. They would ask her about where the best place to get a tattoo was in town, or if it hurt. Or if she was going to get more. Most of the time she would nod and not even respond.

"Really, you're seriously getting one?" she'd say once in a while, staring at them with her dark eyes until they squirmed.

Although she was pretty scary looking, I knew she really wasn't that bad. David didn't need to tell me. I watched her slow, gray energy move around her. She wasn't full of life, but she wasn't dark either. The way it floated around her reminded me of Dr. Mortimer's energy, the way it looked right after he had killed Nathaniel. I figured that Mo probably carried a deep sadness of some sort with her, buried behind walls.

I finished ringing up the women. They were just buying beans. I was glad that we wouldn't have to wait for them while they finished drinks.

"Thanks, hon," the older one said, pulling up her hood and heading out into the rain. After the bells rang and they were gone, Mo came up to me.

"I hate that *hon* shit," she said.

"Me, too," I said, smiling.

I boxed up the remaining pastries and left it on the counter. Mike donated them to the homeless shelters and every morning they came by to pick up the day-olds right before we opened.

I grabbed a pound of the dark roast espresso beans from the shelf, and put it next to the register so I wouldn't forget to take it home. It was one of the perks of the job. Free beans every week.

It was pouring outside now, heavy drops pounding on the roof in a steady rhythm.

"Let's call it," Mo said. I nodded and she turned the sign over and brought down the blinds.

Mo cleared out the cash register, counted the money, and took it in the back to put away in the safe. When she came back out, we both started working on the espresso bar. We were working again side by side in complete silence, and once again I caught myself looking over at her arms.

They really were striking. Both arms were covered in ink. Some of the tattoos were large, some small, all of them making some sort of statement. I made out a large heart with a crack down the middle, a girl holding an electric guitar, and a large cross.

My eyes had stayed on them too long.

"Thinking of getting one?" she said. I inhaled suddenly when our eyes met.

I smiled awkwardly and shook my head. I tried to think of something smart to say, a good way to describe them that didn't sound like those nervous women. They weren't exactly beautiful, but they did have an interesting charm.

"They're so intricate," I sputtered out finally, knowing how dumb it sounded.

She looked down at the girl holding the guitar.

"That's supposed to be me playing," she said, pointing. "And that's the name of our band under it."

I moved a little closer and studied it.

"No Mercy," I said. "Cool."

She grabbed the broom for a final sweep around the store as I finished washing out the half and half canisters. It was crazy. In all the months since I had been working at Back Street, I realized that we had just had our first conversation.

We finished up, closing only about 15 minutes earlier than usual. I phoned Kate, got her voicemail, and left a quick message telling her I was heading home.

"You on tomorrow?" Mo asked, as we stood in the rain while she locked the front doors.

"No," I said.

"Later," she said.

I watched as she took off across the asphalt, darting over the deep puddles. As I ran behind her, I realized that my Jeep was the only car parked in the lot and that Mo was walking. I caught sight of her sprinting away into the dark, wet night, turning off on Bond Street before I had a chance to offer her a ride home in the hard rain.

# Chapter 6

The highway was empty and I stepped down on the accelerator, pushing the Jeep just past 65. I unrolled the window and let the warm air fill the car. It was a beautiful day with only a few clouds in the far distance, the sun high, looking down across the open desert.

I hadn't been out to the Badlands in a long time, hadn't even been on this highway going east and cutting through the high desert in years. The hiking trail was only about 18 miles from town, but the landscape felt so removed and different from what I was used to. Gone were the mountain views and buttes and pine trees. This mostly flat, lonely land was filled with rocks and junipers and sagebrush and assorted desert grasses under a big sky.

It was Friday and I felt lucky to have the day off. And although Ty had to work, he didn't start until five which meant that we had the entire afternoon to hike.

"Let me pick you up so we can drive there together," he said when I called him.

"No, I'll be fine," I said, sticking to my plan. "I want to stop by Big Sky Park first and get in some practice."

Big Sky was where I played soccer most of the time and it had six soccer fields, baseball diamonds, and even a bicycle motocross course. It was a great place to practice shooting, especially during weekday mornings and afternoons before school let out.

"I can come along and practice with you," he said.

"It's right on the way, Ty. I'll just meet you at the trailhead. I'll be fine. Really. I'll call you when I finish."

"Okay," he said, sounding a little frustrated. "I have to pick up my check and stop at the bank, so I'll be there about one."

"See you then," I said.

Ty had started working over at 10 Barrel. There hadn't been too much work up at the mountain this season, so he got a part-time job at the popular pub and brewery over on Galveston Avenue. But he seemed happy. Bend was becoming known as a beer hotspot across the country and Ty was pretty excited about having a job in the industry, even if he was a waiter. He was hoping they would teach him about the brewing aspect of the business. I was glad that he was still planning on working as a river guide this summer.

I turned up Kathleen Edwards as she sang about breakfast and monsters, slowing down when I saw the small sign for the Badlands. A minute later I pulled into the dirt lot by the Flatiron trailhead.

There was only one other car in the lot, an older Toyota 4 Runner. I was surprised Ty hadn't beaten me here.

I had forgotten that it was never too crowded out here. Most people went up to the mountains or hiked along the river trail. Maybe it was too quiet for them. It suited me just fine. You could hear yourself think. Maybe that's what kept people away.

I jumped out, my legs a little sore from my run so I did some stretching while I waited. It had been a solid practice, my speed was getting better and so was my stamina. My shots were on target, low and hard, hitting the back of the net most of the time like they meant business.

I heard the sound of a car on the highway and then saw the dust rise behind his pickup. Ty parked next to me.

"Hey, Abby," he said, jumping out and slamming the door.

My insides churned like they always did when I saw him for the first time.

"Hey," I said, smiling.

He walked up to me and pulled up his sunglasses briefly showing me his eyes while he smiled. It was an inside joke. I was always on him about how those particular glasses he loved to wear all year drove me crazy because I could never see his eyes and never knew where to look when we were talking.

He reached over and pulled me close, kissing me softly on the lips.

"Sorry I'm late," he said, afterwards. "I didn't want you waiting here by yourself like that. You should have stayed over at the park."

"I literally just got here. Seriously. Look, the Jeep is still warm," I said, putting my hand on the hood.

Ty sighed and put his hand on top on mine and let it sit there for a minute.

"Didn't mean to go all Christoph Waltz on you earlier," he said before looking away. "I just, you know, worry sometimes."

I studied his energy. It moved like it always did, fast and light, dancing playfully around him. He smiled and leaned toward me, kissing me again.

"I have extra water if you need it," he said, swinging his backpack over his shoulder. I grabbed my pack from the backseat and locked the door.

"Ready?"

"Oh, yeah," he said. "Been looking forward to it all morning."

He was wearing cargo shorts and a dark T-shirt and a fleece jacket tied around his waist. He was letting his hair grow out and it was becoming shaggy and long, touching the tips of his shoulders. He had a surfer thing going.

We started walking on the trail which led to a sign and a board with a map. After studying it for a minute, we started walking down the dusty path that snaked through the brush.

"So are we running or walking the five miles?" he asked. Ty was all about trail running lately.

"How about we walk fast?" I said.

"Perfect," he said, taking my hand. "I still can't believe nobody's out here. It's kind of nice, really."

I looked around.

"It's always like this," I said. "Kate and I used to come out here to bike sometimes, years ago."

"How is Kate by the way? It feels like I haven't seen her in a while."

"She seems okay. Painting."

"Which room now?" he asked.

"Bathroom. She's running out of walls though, so she might be heading to your house soon," I said.

I laughed nervously and hoped I hadn't insulted him because the house he was renting was, actually, in dire need of a good paint job. Ty was living in one of those inexpensive, tiny places, back behind the Old Mill and not far from the river. He lived there with Brad, a childhood friend from Montana who had recently moved to Bend and was hoping to land a job as a river guide this summer.

"Whatever Kate needs," Ty said as we walked. "My walls are her walls."

"Only say it if you mean it," I said.

"I mean it."

A warm breeze hit us as we picked up the pace, walking up a small hill and then back down the other side.

"Maybe we can talk her into coming out for a beer or dinner this weekend," he said, after a few minutes. "She works too hard."

It struck me as odd that he said that, but then I remembered that Ty really hadn't known Kate that long at all, even if they had become fast, good friends. He had picked us up from the airport on that cold winter afternoon following the kidnapping. He stayed every night for a week, bringing us dinner, going to the store, picking up work for Kate at the newspaper so she didn't have to leave me. He had been incredible and helped us get through those first few tough weeks.

"Well, Kate's not really working like she used to," I finally said.

It seemed important to me, for some reason, for him to know her better.

"You should have seen her before, before all that happened. She hardly ever came home, worked all weekend. She was an insane workaholic, filing twice as many stories as the other reporters. The kidnapping changed her. Sometimes I think it changed her more than it did me. She only goes in for the basic 40 hours a week now and spends the rest of her time fixing up the house. It's kind of weird."

He was quiet for a moment.

"She's just trying to cope with everything," he said. "That was a terrible thing you went through. And even though it happened to you, worrying is a bitch. It really takes it out of you."

A wave of guilt washed over me as I thought about how I hadn't told Ty everything. He knew the basic story, about how Nathaniel Mortimer wanted to continue his research on me and about how his brother had accidently shot him. And about Jack Martin, of course. But there was still so much Ty didn't know about me and maybe that was why I wasn't really sure where we stood in terms of a relationship.

He didn't know about the ghosts I sometimes saw walking around town, or about seeing Jesse, Emma, or Annabelle. He didn't know anything about those visions I once had of Nathaniel killing people. Or about the energy I saw swirling around people that gave me an insight into their moods. I wanted to tell him, some of the time, but other times it felt like he knew enough about the crazy side of my life. I didn't want to scare him away, I guess. But now I was wondering. I was wondering if there was any chance for a relationship that had such secrets.

Ty checked his odometer that he wore on his wrist and then grabbed my hand again as we walked on the trail, the warm sun strong in our faces. It felt great to be out here, on the edge of summer, on the edge of other good things.

"I'm going this weekend to get my board," he said.

"Cool."

Ty had been saving up to buy a paddleboard to take out in the mornings on the Deschutes.

We walked a little farther.

I wondered if I was falling in love with him. I could feel it in my stomach and in my knees, always wobbly whenever I saw him. But I told myself I wasn't ready to get serious yet, and I told him too, regularly. He always said it was okay, that he was happy with how things were and that he could wait. But I knew things would have to move forward at some point, and probably pretty soon. And the truth was that sometimes I wanted them to as well.

I knew my hesitation with Ty had to do with Jesse. I was better about it than before, much better, and had been really trying to let Jesse go. But it was nowhere near easy. I still loved him and I wondered if that feeling had to die before I could move ahead with Ty.

But other times it felt like it was really possible to love two people at the same time, which was surprising. I thought that if you really loved someone with your whole heart, there wasn't any room to love someone else. But lately I wasn't so sure.

After a couple of miles, we climbed up a small ridge and stopped, looking out across the quiet desert.

"Amazing," Ty said.

It felt like we were the only ones around, although just as I thought that, we saw a couple of bikes coming toward us, down the trail. They must have been heading back to the parking lot and I was guessing that the 4 Runner belonged to them.

Ty put his arm around me.

"I love being with you, Abby," he said, his eyes hidden behind his shades.

"Me, too," I said, knowing that it didn't make too much sense. I hoped he knew what I meant.

We walked back on the trail and I thought about David. He must be right. Ty was my beautiful boyfriend.

In another minute the bikes were right on top of us. We stepped aside and let them pass.

I saw something else moving behind us in the distance down the trail. At first I thought it might have been wildlife, maybe a mule deer or coyote, but after a few seconds it became clear that it was a person, another hiker.

We reached a large fire pit that I hadn't noticed when we were coming in. It was filled with old burned-out coffee and bean cans.

"Strange," I said. "Who would sit around and burn up hundreds of old cans?"

Ty picked up one of the larger ones. It looked like a relic from an ancient civilization, although I did notice that it had the letters Y-U-B-A-N bubbling over the charred metal.

"Hey, don't you think this would be very cool as a vase? You could put flowers in them."

"Really?" I asked. I couldn't see it, they looked kind of *junkyardy* to me.

"Yeah. It'll look cool," he said, kicking a few around with his foot. "Artsy. You'll see. Do you think Kate would like one?"

I thought of the new leather furniture and lamps.

"Well, I don't think it's exactly her style," I said.

"I'm bringing back a few. If she doesn't want one, I'll use them all. We need to do a little decorating. This will be perfect."

I made sure not to laugh as Ty picked up a few cans and I helped, careful not to cut myself and end up with a severed finger or lockjaw. Maybe he was right. Maybe with some flowers in them, they would look good. Maybe.

We walked back down the trail with our cans, stopping for water once. Again, I saw movement behind us and this time it caused my heart to race. I was always so jittery lately, even with Ty by my side.

But I settled down when I saw that the stranger behind us was just a kid. He was still kind of far, but I could make out his Guns N' Roses T-shirt. It didn't make any sense for him to be out here all alone. I supposed he could have lived in one of the ranches I saw when I drove in or maybe he belonged to a band of can-burning nomads.

He hung back, and never caught up or passed us. In a little while, I saw the roof of Ty's truck up ahead.

"Bummer I have to work tonight," Ty said, grabbing my hand again.

"Yeah," I said. "So how is your schedule going to be when we start back on the river?"

He shrugged.

"I've told them I have to start back at the end of May and I'll have to cut down on my hours, but they still want to give me 30. It might be too many, especially when we're in high season. What about you? Have you told Mike yet?"

I shook my head.

"No," I said. "Not yet."

I had planned to tell him, but somehow the time never quite seemed right. I was glad that I was asked to come back and didn't want to say, oh, and by the way, I can't work too much in the summer. Summer was a busy time for all the businesses downtown and I was worried he would let me go and hire someone else.

"I better do that soon," I said. "But I don't start guiding for a few months still. Rebecca said she won't need me until the middle of June so I have some time."

Since I was the last hire, I was scheduled to start late, when the season was in full gear and the kids were out of school.

"Did you sign your contract yet?" he asked.

"Yeah, I went in last week."

I hadn't told Kate yet. No point in starting with all that again so soon.

"You?"

"No, not yet. I want to bring Brad along when I sign so he can meet everybody. See if I can talk him up a little before the try out. He was a great river guide back home. I'm hoping they'll just hire him on the spot."

We put the old cans in the back of the truck.

"I guess I'll just pick up my can when I see you," I said, smiling.

"Uh-huh, I see how it is," Ty said and then leaned down to kiss me again. His lips were tangy, like he had been

42

walking next to the sea. I was hoping the lurking kid wasn't around watching.

"That was nice," I whispered.

"Right back at you. Okay, I'll follow you out. Drive safe. Hey, we're still on for a movie tomorrow night, right?"

"Yeah," I said. "You pick it. It's the least I can do after that elephant fiasco."

"I'll try not to make it a revenge thing," he said. "But I can't make any promises."

We pulled out of the parking lot and out onto the highway, my heart thumping fast and wild.

But in a good way.

# Chapter 7

I struggled in the black water. I held my breath, fighting to reach the surface. But I couldn't hold on. Desperate for air, I opened my mouth, the water stinging as it washed through my lungs.

I woke up gasping.

"I'm home," I said to myself.

I forced myself out of bed, woozy and half asleep, and went to check on the backyard.

No water.

No waves or swells or docks.

I wasn't on an island, in a strange house. I was home, in my room.

The moon was large, not quite full but luminous, lighting up the cloudless dark sky and everything else. I could see the new bird fountain over by the pine trees and the rake and hoe that Kate had left outside, leaning against the side of the house.

I glanced back at the clock, angry that it was only a little past two. I had just fallen asleep half an hour ago. Soft music that I had programmed to play for an hour was still coming from my iPod.

I stared into the night. I was groggy and my stomach felt like I was standing on a lake in the middle of a storm.

I couldn't get those images out of my mind. That large mansion surrounded by water, the secluded island, the motor boat coming after me. The drowning pool he had tried to kill me in. The moments when he strapped me onto the stretcher and lowered it down into the water. The handful of scientists standing around in white lab coats taking notes on the experiment, which was supposed to involve killing me and then bringing me back to life. The glint of the sharp needle he held out as he waited for me to die.

I felt the horror pulsate through me body just like I was there again, and I suddenly jerked away from the window and ran over to the bathroom, the vomit, warm and bitter, barely making it into the toilet bowl.

Everything had come up. The pizza I had with Ty earlier, the soda and popcorn I ate during the movie. The ice cream. Everything.

I wasn't going to cry though. There had been enough tears. Too many and I wasn't going to do that anymore. I was a survivor and it was time to move on. I sat shaking on the bathroom floor for a moment before pulling myself up and soaking my face in the sink. I toweled off and flushed the remains of my fear away, catching my reflection in the mirror.

Kate was right. I wasn't looking so good. Too pale, my face thin, too thin even with all those pastries, with those dark circles under swollen eyes.

I looked like an experiment. I looked like something Nathaniel Mortimer had created in his lab. Not fully alive, and not fully dead.

Maybe Messi didn't need to rest, pouting whenever his coach even thought about giving him a game off, but I did. I wasn't going to make it if I didn't start sleeping soon.

I shuffled back to bed and put on my robe tightly, scanning the backyard one more time before heading out to the living room to make the rounds. I walked softly, creeping past Kate's door. It was dark in her room and I was glad she wasn't up.

First I checked the security system. It was on, the bright light glowing out into the black living room. I sat on the cold leather sofa and listened to the sounds that are amplified by darkness. It was windy out, and I watched the moving shadows of the pine trees in front of the house through the curtains, heard their long branches brushing up against the windows. The house creaked in the gusts.

After a few minutes, I got up and checked the front door. It was locked, like we had left it before we went to bed. The sliding glass door in the kitchen was still locked, too. So were all the windows.

I had made Kate take my window off the security system. I needed to be able to open it, to be able to feel the dry air on my skin. She had argued, but I was adamant about it. I had to be able to get to it in those lonely, dark hours, especially after a nightmare.

I promised her I would keep the window locked though, that I would be careful to never leave it open. Sometimes I heard her creep into my room, checking it.

I wandered back over to Kate's door. It was closed, but I now saw a light bleeding out from the cracks. I put my ear up to it, but it was quiet.

I headed back over to the sofa and sat down, my feet cold on the floor, listening to the noises of the night.

# Chapter 8

"He was such an ass," David said, talking about his old boss at a restaurant that had closed last month. "You just can't treat people like that."

I emptied the tip jar and put it in a plastic pouch under the change holder in the register. A woman walked in and ordered a decaf mocha and before I even mentioned it, I heard David slapping out the old coffee grounds and starting her drink.

It was Monday night and it had been busy for hours at Back Street, with people coming in and out all evening and a book club in the corner by the gas fireplace talking in librarian voices but then occasionally breaking out in loud laughter. The group came in every week and we were getting to know them and for the most part they were friendly. Mike liked them because he said it gave the place an intellectual vibe. Plus, he said, they ordered a lot of coffee.

I didn't read books too often, hardly ever really, but was impressed by how much passion they all had as they discussed their opinions about the different characters and plots. I couldn't even imagine being excited about reading like they were. When I thought of books, I flashed back to high school and those long, old, boring classics that Mrs.

Willows assigned to us in English. I never thought that reading could actually be fun.

I walked by the group and wiped down the nearby tables. They were arguing about the next selection. One of the younger women wanted the group to read a new bestseller about gray shades or something, but some of the others said it was pornographic and refused to even buy it.

It had been a pretty fun time with David. It was just the two of us for most of the night and he talked nonstop about all his old jobs and old bosses, before starting a rant about his old boyfriends. Then he told me about his dreams, about how he had been taking acting lessons since he was a kid.

"So, what, you want to star in musicals?" I said.

"Child, please," he said, shaking his head. "I'm not a total cliché, you know. Strictly serious acting, Abby. No singing and no dancing."

"I'm sorry," I said, hoping I hadn't offended him. "And I'm glad. I hate musicals."

"I couldn't agree more. I mean, shoot me now."

He told me he was going to try out for a part at 2nd Street Theater, going after the lead role, and then started reciting lines. He was pretty good. I promised him I'd go to opening night if he got the part.

The place started clearing out at about 8:30 and I was hopeful that we could get out on time. I started cleaning, sweeping the floor and pulling the scattered chairs back over to their tables.

"So where did you meet this Ty guy?" David asked, wiping down the countertops.

"On the river last summer," I said.

"The river?" he said. "What were you two doing on the river?"

I told him. I guess he hadn't expected it, me being a river guide. Although we had had a lot of conversations,

David was the one who did most of the talking, which was okay by me. Pretty much the only things he knew about me were that I had a sister who worked at the newspaper and a boyfriend with light hair. Not much more.

"River guides?" he said.

"Yeah. You know. Taking groups down the rapids on the Deschutes."

Still, he looked blank and I shook my head.

Sometimes I wondered if David ever went outside. Whenever I talked about hiking or biking or skiing, that same empty expression crawled across his perpetually pale never-been-in-the-sun face. I had the feeling that he never stepped outside except to walk to and from his car. He kind of lived like a vampire, partying in the clubs all night and sleeping it off most of the day.

"Come on, now," I said, a little too sarcastically. "River guides."

"Abby Craig, don't be snide," he said. "I'm just trying to figure out where the heck the rapids even are on the river, that's all. I've only seen it calm and gentle."

I had forgotten that David had moved here just a year or so ago and that maybe he had lived in a city back home. He probably had only noticed the river gliding by at Drake Park, near downtown.

"There's plenty of whitewater on the Deschutes," I said. "We launch upriver, about ten miles from town."

He nodded and smiled and I was glad I hadn't hurt his feelings.

"Hey, you should come with us on a run this summer."

He ran his fingers through his hair and considered it for half a second, at most.

"Rapids? Me?" he said. "Thank you very much, but no. Can't take those kinds of chances. Plus I bet you'd make me don those dreadful bright puffy orange vests that make you look fat. No. Not for me."

Soft, jazzy music played in the background. It was always so different working nights with David compared to Mo. Calmer. And more fun.

I heard the bells on the door and saw that an older man who wore a plaid hat had walked in. David helped him, taking his money and then moving quickly to the machines and pulling a shot of espresso. The old guy threw it back in one gulp and left.

"So does that mean you're quitting here?" David asked.

I cringed. Mentioning the river guide job had been a mistake. I had forgotten that David loved to gossip and it would only be a matter of time now before Mike would find out about my plans.

"No, I don't want to quit. I like it here," I said. "A lot. I'm hoping I can do both, but I'll have to see what Mike says. I just haven't told him yet."

"Hmm," David said, stacking dirty mugs on a tray and taking them to the dishwasher in the back.

There was no point in getting him to promise not to say anything. I knew that even if he did, the news would slip out anyway. David's friendly, chatty nature was one of the things I really liked about him. But what was good was also bad. It was my own doing. As long as I was in such a talkative mood, I should tell Mike. Maybe during my next shift or I could even send him an email.

At exactly nine, I turned over the sign hanging off the door and by 9:10 the last of the book club members left. I called Kate and left a message while David took the money out of the register, counted it, and took it back to the safe. I then took the broom, dustpan, and a stack of napkins to the closet and quickly checked the week's schedule. David wasn't working for two days and I was hoping that maybe he would forget about my summer plans by then.

"Well," he said as I waited by the door for him to lock up. He put on his coat, the keys jiggling in his hand.

"I guess I won't see you until the weekend, River Guide Abby Craig."

I would write to Mike later, when I got home.

# Chapter 9

I decided to head out to Big Sky, even if I didn't have a full hour. I wanted to practice my shooting and there was nothing like shooting into real goals.

I strolled out to the grass and inhaled the cool air, dropping my keys and mace in my pocket and pushing the ball out in front of me. I was wishing I had a little more time, wishing I hadn't picked up when Mike had called and asked if I could come in early. But 45 minutes of practice was better than nothing and I started picking up my speed, keeping my eyes focused out in front of me and not on the ball.

Except for a few people over at the dog park, I had the place to myself. It was strange seeing all six fields empty, the only sound a crow cawing as it circled above me overhead.

I started taking some shots, making most of them, sprinting in after them in case there was a rebound. One shot missed the net, rattling hard off the crossbar and ricocheting back over in my general direction. I jumped up and put it back in off my forehead.

I took off again downfield and started working on my conditioning.

I was following a fitness program that I had found on-line a few months ago. My speed was faster than ever before. Even before the accident. As I ran I gave thanks for being able to play again, this game I loved so much. It was hard to believe that there was a time not so long ago when I felt I would never be out here again. But now it all seemed possible. The 2015 World Cup. The 2016 Olympics. Why not? Me and Alex Morgan leading the team in scoring. Why not?

Driven by the boundless possibilities, or the lack of oxygen to my brain, I pushed myself even harder.

I could hear the barking of a dog in the distance, his howl carried by the wind, past the junipers, past the goal posts and fields, and into the surrounding desert.

After a few minutes, I fell back into an easy trot and looked around again. There were a few women with dogs in the distance and an older man now juggling one field over. A park maintenance employee was next to the bathrooms, emptying trashcans.

Out here in the fresh air, the long, sleepless night almost seemed to be part of someone else's life. But then I caught myself yawning. I had to try something new. Whatever I was doing wasn't working.

I did a few more field-length sprints, focusing on taking quality shots as I closed in on goal. Then I worked on free kicks and penalties. I had read that the hardest place for a goalkeeper to make a save on PKs was high in the corners. I aimed for the spot just below where the post met the crossbar. Of course, some players aimed right for the goalie, knowing that chances were good that he would lunge in one direction or the other. Most experienced keepers don't want to just stand there, hoping that the ball will come right at them. They want to earn their keep, so they try to read the shooter's mind and guess right. Or left. I practiced some shots straight down the middle.

On one of these attempts, I missed badly, kicking the ball off the side of my instep, sending it spiraling high and wide, flying perfectly in the left top shelf corner.

At one point a middle-aged man came by with his crazy Labrador, cutting across the field. He didn't have it on a leash and it started chasing after me.

"Sorry," the guy said, whistling and then yelling and then whistling again. The dog ignored him, and ran off and disappeared into the brush.

I checked my watch and saw I only had a few minutes left, so I ran downfield full speed to the opposite goal line and turned around and sprinted back for one more shot. For all the marbles. But as I looked up toward the goal, I saw that someone was in it, pretending to be a keeper.

I picked up the gauntlet and kept coming. If somebody wanted to try and stop me from scoring, good luck to them. I crossed midfield and thought about where I would put my shot.

As I got closer, I saw that it was a kid between the posts, not quite a teenager. He must have been with the man and the crazy dog, but had stayed behind to play a little soccer. I was glad. I could use the practice with a live goalkeeper and started visualizing how bad I wanted to burn him.

He was light on his feet, bouncing gingerly, taking a few steps away from the line and holding out his hands, palms facing toward me. He seemed to know what he was doing. At first he hung back, but then he came out to close the angle. Smart, I thought.

*I'll just fake left and go right around him*, I thought. *Or fake right and go left. Okay, left.* And then... *Sure, why not?*

I decided to do neither. Instead I would chip the ball over him. That would show him.

I closed in, noticing he wasn't smiling or even looking up at me. He kept his focus razor sharp on my feet and the ball. I thought about how much force to use, not too hard and not too soft, and how far under the ball to get.

*Now*, I thought.

"Not today, kid," I said out loud as I stepped into it. I lobbed it over him just right and watched it sail through the air, a work of art now more than a ball. But as I stood there admiring my skill, the boy somehow backed up and jumped high in the air, putting himself in position to make an awesome save.

"Damn," I said under my breath.

The ball was heading straight for his hands. There was no way he could miss it.

But he did.

I stood there, breathing hard, amazed that the ball got past him, almost like it had gone right through him, and bounced into the goal.

Adrenaline suddenly rushed through my body as I realized *what* he was.

He looked up at me slowly and I staggered back. His large eyes had deep, black circles around them, his lips as pale as his face. I could see scratches and scars and bruises all over his arms. His face had a deep gash on the right side that ran down from his eyebrow to his neck.

He was wearing jeans and a familiar Guns N' Roses T-shirt.

There was no ducking away or turning or hiding from this ghost. Our eyes locked and he knew that I had seen him. He stared at me somberly with washed out eyes, waiting.

"Abby," he said.

I was numb with fear and I couldn't move. I couldn't run.

"Abby," he whispered again, almost prayer like, his haunting voice carried by the wind to my ears. "Help."

I heard the loose dog behind me again, breathing hard as it ran up, barking as it circled, the owner still chasing after it and calling its name.

When I turned back toward the net, the ghost boy was gone.

# Chapter 10

He knew me.

The ghost knew my name.

I sat in the Jeep with the doors locked, the windows rolled up tight, trying to shake off the chills that ran up and down my back and stared out at the empty field.

It wasn't like I hadn't seen a ghost before. Or that I had stopped seeing them. I still saw them around town sometimes, walking along the sidewalks, sitting at tables in empty restaurants, walking in parks. But I never made eye contact, never acknowledged them even if I had a feeling they wanted to talk to me.

And so far, it had worked out fine. Since I had been back from the island, the only ghost I talked to was Jesse.

But somehow, I was too late in figuring it out with this kid. He saw that I saw him.

And he knew my name.

Even though I was getting used to seeing the dead, they still scared me. And I had never seen a kid ghost before. It left a sad feeling inside and I wondered how he had died. By the looks of the scars and cuts, it seemed certain that it wasn't natural causes.

The dog and his owner finally left. I watched the goal for a while longer, wondering if the ghost would return now that it was quiet, but he didn't come back.

I drank the rest of my water and tried to calm my nerves. I didn't really know what to do and then I thought about my last conversation with Jesse.

"Whatever you do, Craigers, don't make any eye contact with them," he said as we walked along the frozen river. It was in late February and a light snow had left a thin layer of white on everything. I was out for a run and I found Jesse in the park, standing next to the river.

We stood and watched the ducks fly in and land on the water and then slide across the icy parts like it was a skating rink.

"Don't even look in their direction. That way, the ghosts will leave you alone."

I didn't mind his advice. Truthfully, I was perfectly content talking to just one ghost. But it had felt right helping Annabelle and her family and I wondered if I should be helping more of them.

"But maybe it's what I'm supposed to do," I said.

"No, it's not your job," Jesse said. "Look, every ghost has a sad story. And there are a lot of them, trust me. You can't waste all your energy being pulled into their problems. That's not why you came back. If you let them, they'll end up sucking the life out of you."

"That's harsh," I said, tugging at a tree branch that was covered in snow. All the plants and trees were a stark white. "I'm just saying that me seeing ghosts and helping them, well, maybe that's the good in all this."

He sighed and shook his head.

"The good in all of this is that you're still alive," he said. "And that you have an opportunity to live your life. For you, not for them."

He stared at me, his eyes slicing into mine. It seemed like we always ended up arguing when I talked about the ghosts I sometimes saw.

"I know that and I didn't mean it that way," I said. "I meant that it could be another good thing that came out of my accident. That I can help people."

"They're not people," Jesse said bluntly. "Not any-more."

"But when I helped Annabelle, I also helped her son, who is very much alive."

After I mentioned it, I wished I hadn't. It still bothered me that while we had been able to locate Annabelle's body at the bottom of the Deschutes River, we hadn't been able to help solve her murder. But at least her family now knew what had happened to her.

"Craigers, the ghosts need to move on," he said. "It's not good for you and it's not good for them to be staying in this world, so focused on their past."

I sighed.

"We all leave this world with unfinished business, re-grets, things we want to set right," he said. "And it always comes too soon. But when it does come, that's it. It's time to move on. That's what they need to realize. You need to listen to me and stay away from them."

"Come on," I said. "Don't be so dramatic. Not all the stories are of murders and brutal deaths. What about your dad? I helped him. I think I helped him a lot."

I was excited when we went over to the motorcycle shop and I told Mr. Stone that I could see and talk to his dead son. Jesse was so sure that his dad wouldn't believe me, but he was wrong. Although Mr. Stone didn't say much or ask any questions, he listened to everything Jesse told me to tell him with watery eyes and a kind smile. Jesse told him how much he loved him and missed him and that he was sorry about the accident.

Jesse smiled suddenly, like he was remembering the visit too. He stopped and took my hand and kissed it.

"I know," he said. "And I loved talking to my dad like that with you. You're right. It helped him. And it helped me too."

I nodded.

"But these others, they'll suck the life out of you, Craigers. They don't care. And they know about you now, about how you can see them. Some are looking for you."

Goose bumps covered my arms.

"What? What do you mean they're looking for me?"

My heart jumped into a sudden, crazy fast pace.

"Just listen to what I'm saying. Walk past them and you'll be fine. Focus on what you want to do with your life."

I stared out at the soccer field. The ghost still hadn't come back.

It wasn't as simple as the *see no ghosts, hear no ghosts, speak to no ghosts* approach Jesse wanted me to take. Maybe I had a say in it, a choice to make. Maybe it wasn't my destiny to help them, but if one of them came to me asking for help, it wasn't in my nature to just turn away without a good reason.

I wasn't sure what the ghost boy wanted from me, but I had the feeling he would tell me.

I turned on the car, cranked the heater, and sat back.

And remembered.

It wasn't the first time. The ghost had been at the Badlands that day. He was on the trail, following Ty and me. It was the same kid that I saw when we were hiking.

A fresh set of goose bumps ran down my arms. I pulled out of the lot. It was stormy up ahead, dark clouds gathering, the darkness looming.

# Chapter 11

It had been crowded and super busy at Back Street the entire day. Working through the lunch hour was never as fun or relaxing as the night shifts, and I missed David. I even missed Mo.

Kate stopped by to say hello but didn't stay for too long. I wasn't able to take my break with her, and she seemed preoccupied. There was a constant line that always threatened to spill out the door, no matter how fast I took the orders. The longer wait and lack of seating made tempers short, causing some to leave in a huff.

And even though it was busy, the hours snailed by. I was looking forward to the rest of the week, working nights and seeing David.

There were a few other employees who worked during the day that I didn't know that well. One was a woman who constantly talked about her daughter. And then there was Lyle, a photographer who had his work in a few of the galleries around town. He took a lot of nature shots. Mike had a few of them framed up on the walls over the tables. They were really good, shots of a climbers scaling Monkey Face at Smith Rock, Broken Top at sunrise, a fly fisherman casting at Hosmer Lake.

But I didn't talk too much to either of them, just to Mike, who had been in a good mood all day, like most days.

After talking with David that night, I had sent Mike an email telling him about my summer river plans. I was worried that he might be mad or something, especially after I had disappeared on him at the end of last year. But he wasn't. He asked me what the hours were like and I told him.

"We'll make it work," he said, making a fresh pot of Costa Rica blend. "No problem. You're a great employee and we'll figure it out."

I was glad. It's not like my big plan in life was to work here forever, but it felt right for now and it was nice to be appreciated.

I tried to focus on what I was doing, but my thoughts drifted back to the ghost I had seen out on the soccer field. I couldn't help wondering about how he died.

He had said he needed help, but I didn't know who he was or what he wanted. There was nothing I could do but wait. And in a strange way, I was hoping it wouldn't be for too much longer. I didn't like being stalked and would rather just deal with his problem, whatever that might be.

By the last hour of my shift, I was exhausted and wishing it would slow down so Mike would send me home. I was ready for an afternoon nap. But there was no way. It was still wall to wall customers and I ended up staying later than I had been scheduled for.

At just past six o'clock, I stepped outside, into the parking lot to finally head home. The sky was a light gray, all in clouds, but it was a little warmer than earlier. I saw David, his tires burning rubber as he swerved in and parked right next to me, a little too close.

He was late, like he usually was.

"Hello and goodbye, Abby Craig," he said, jumping out of the old Camaro and brushing by me.

"Hey, wait, how did the audition go?" I asked. I was glad that I had remembered.

"Nailed it! Just got the call. Just call me Leo DiCaprio from now on," he said.

"That's awesome, David," I said. I leaned in and gave him a quick, awkward hug. He smiled and his eyes twinkled when I looked back at him.

"Congratulations. You really must have wowed them."

"Yeah, I think I did," he said, backing up toward the store. "So you're coming, right? It's at 2nd Street, but not until July."

"You know it," I said.

"Good. I'll get you and your sister in the front row. Oh, and BB can come too, if he wants."

"That would be awesome," I said.

He smiled before running into Back Street.

When I walked into the house, I found Kate sitting on the sofa and watching TV, already in her sweats and T-shirt, hair up and wearing an apron. I was still getting used to her new schedule, but I liked it. It was nice having her home for dinner every night.

"Hey, Abby," she said, getting up and meeting me at the door.

"Wow, it smells great in here," I said.

Still, it was a strange moment. Me coming home from work and Kate making dinner. Like everything was upside down and mixed up in the universe.

I walked into the kitchen and saw a large metal pot on the backburner of the stove and a stack of dishes in the sink. I was starving and it smelled amazing.

"Hungry?" she asked.

I nodded.

"I'll be back in a minute," I said.

I went to my bedroom, threw down my stuff, and washed up.

When I walked back out, the television was off, Miles Davis blowing his horn in the background. Two plates of Linguini Alfredo were on the table, with crusty slices of garlic bread in a basket between the dishes.

"Wow, thanks," I said as I sat down.

It was one of Kate's best dishes and it had been a long time since she made it. She grated some fresh parmesan over the pasta and then sat down, pouring herself some wine.

"Want a glass?" she asked.

"No, I'm okay," I said. "Soda's fine."

We sat and ate, mostly quiet, both of us lost in deep thought.

"That was delicious," I said for the fifth time when we had finished. But I couldn't help it. It really was.

"Good, I'm glad you liked it," she said. "It's kind of fun to cook again. But really, Abby, I miss your dishes. You're really good and I hope you have some plans to start back soon."

I hadn't cooked much since the kidnapping. I wasn't sure why. Maybe it had to do with Simon, one of the scientists on the island who had showed me how to make risotto and talked about food like it was a religion. Or maybe I was just too busy.

Sometimes I wondered how Simon was doing. I was pretty sure I'd see him at the trial. Kate had learned off the record that he was in witness protection, hidden away, waiting to testify. I was happy for him, his heart never seemed into holding me captive, and in the end he tried to help me escape. I wondered if he was working as a chef somewhere.

"You should invite Ty over. He must not even know how great of a cook you are."

She was right. I hadn't made him anything other than a few batches of cookies.

I got up and started clearing the plates.

"Oh, let's leave them for a little while," Kate said, picking up her glass and walking over to the sofa.

It had taken me too long to figure out something was wrong. She had been too quiet over dinner and now leaving the dishes for later made it obvious.

I grabbed another soda from the fridge and followed her over to the sofa.

# Chapter 12

"So what's up?" I asked.

She pulled her eyes away from the window and leaned in close, lowering her voice.

"Ben," she said. "He finally wrote."

It had been nearly a month since we had heard from Dr. Mortimer, even though Kate wrote to him regularly, giving him updates, asking when he was coming back. But he had taken his brother's death hard and we both worried that it would be something he could never be able to get past.

"What'd he say?" I asked.

Looking at her energy, I could tell it wasn't good.

"He's not coming back."

She sighed heavily. Her face went pale and sad like it always did now when she talked about him. She turned her head to the side, staring back out the window. I could see she was holding back tears. We sat quiet for a moment.

"Not yet," I said after a while. "But he will, Kate. He just needs a little time."

It really hadn't been that long. Five months wasn't nearly enough time for Dr. Mortimer to come to terms with the fact that he had shot and killed his younger brother, even if it had been an accident.

Dr. Mortimer never came back to Bend. After helping with my rescue and talking to the police and FBI, he left with his brother's body for Boston, where they had been born and raised. After he buried Nathaniel, he sent in his resignation to the hospital, wrote to Kate telling her that he had to travel for a while to sort everything out, and had an agency close up his house on Awbrey Butte.

"Where is he?" I asked.

"India," Kate said. "He's living in an ashram. And he says he's going to stay there for a while. Years maybe."

That seemed like a good place for him, at least for now. I didn't know too much about those places, but I remembered seeing something on TV once about a man searching for the meaning of life who ended up going to India and finding answers. Dr. Mortimer wouldn't have been able to just come back here and pick up his life. He needed to make peace with what had happened. Because no matter how insane he was, Nathaniel had still been his brother and Dr. Mortimer had killed him.

"At least he's okay, right?" I said.

"I guess he's all right. But he sounds strange. Told me to say hi to you and to tell you again how sorry he is for everything. How you shouldn't have been put through that horror. And that he still feels responsible for not keeping you safe."

I sighed.

I knew from reading his energy that Nathaniel had never felt any guilt about the things he had done, the lives he had ruined, the people he had killed. And there were so many. I was one of the lucky ones. I had gotten away. And yet, here was his brother, who hadn't done anything wrong, feeling guilty. It wasn't right. We had all been trapped in Nathaniel's insanity through no fault of our own. But Dr. Mortimer didn't see it that way.

"He has nothing to be sorry for," I said.

"The sins of the brother I guess," Kate said.

"Tell him next time you write to him. Tell him he doesn't have one thing to be sorry about. I want him to know that I feel that way. It makes me mad that he's feeling responsible for his brother."

It sent chills down my spine thinking about Nathaniel, those strange, almond eyes full of an intensity and excitement about his research. He was so sure of his ideas and his experiments, so positive that he had found a solution to death.

I shivered as I thought of him, his body lying there on the floor that day I had been rescued.

For a long time, I was sure that Nathaniel was wrong about his claim that he was the one who had saved me after I was dead for 44 minutes. I had drowned in a mountain lake and when they brought me into the hospital, I was gone. But Nathaniel was there, with his serum, and he injected me and somehow, soon afterwards, I woke up from death.

I didn't believe it for a long time. But now, after my time on the island, I knew in my heart that it was true. That I was alive only because of the injection. That his serum did, in fact, bring me back to life that terrible night and that it was Nathaniel Mortimer who had saved my life.

It haunted me sometimes, the knowledge that I owed my life to such a man. During the day, I was pretty good about not thinking about it. But in those long, desperate hours after midnight, the thoughts exploded in my head and pinballed inside my skull and I couldn't stop them. I couldn't stop thinking about him.

I looked over at Kate. She was still lost in thought. I picked up the control and flipped it on, finding *Sweet Genius*, a reality show that I liked to watch sometimes.

"That's just life, isn't it?" Kate said "You finally figure out what you want, but then it's too damn late."

"He'll be back, Kate," I said. "He loves you."

I wondered why I had said that, when I knew that sometimes love just wasn't enough.

## Chapter 13

We weren't able to close up on time so I texted Kate to let her know that I would be late.

*Thanks for the heads up. See you soon.*

Sometimes I hated Mike's policy about how if a customer was sitting down and it was closing time, we couldn't ask them to leave. We could start closing up, lock the doors, turn over the sign, but we had to wait patiently until they finished their drinks and left on their own.

Sometimes waiting was tough. I was tired and wanted to go home. And the two women who were engaged in an animated conversation seemed like they were never going to stop talking, even with the chilly glares that Mo sent their way every few minutes.

They also ignored us as we mopped and wiped down tables.

"Time to go," Mo said under her breath, a little louder than I was expecting, as she walked by them and collected a few dirty cups.

But she was right. It was getting late and I found myself zoning out as I stood, staring into space. I was counting the hours that I had slept over the last three nights and had come up with eight. No wonder I was so emotional all day, and had felt like crying over nothing. It must have been all related to lack of sleep.

I had even snapped at Ty earlier, when he called and told me he couldn't come over for dinner on Friday. They had asked him to work that night. It was pretty stupid anyway because I was way too tired to be slaving away on the Bolognese Lasagna I had planned to cook, but I was still upset. I called him back later and apologized about my behavior.

"No biggy," he said. "I'm sorry too. Can't we just do it on Thursday instead?"

"No, that won't work. But how about next week?"

"Perfect," he said.

I yawned again and started emptying trashcans, hoping the two women might finally get that it was time to hit the road. But no hope was needed. Mo, at the end of her rope, walked over and told them that we were closing.

"Screw the policy," she said to me as she walked back over to the counter.

I looked at clock. It was close to ten.

"Bye, girls," the larger woman said as she pushed open the door. Mo didn't answer and I just gave a little wave to their backs.

There were still a few things to do, but we worked well together now. I didn't mind Mo's silences anymore and appreciated that I didn't have to try and think of something to say. It wasn't like that with Mike. I was always stressing about topics when he came up front and we worked next to each other. I decided that it was nice working with Mo after all.

I pulled down the blinds while Mo turned up a song by Rural Demons, a local band that sounded like a cross between a young Steve Earle and Edgar Allan Poe. She counted out the register. She was fast and took the money back to the safe.

I still didn't know much about Mo, but David could be counted on to pass along any gossip he heard about her. Like about how she had just broken up with the lead singer in her band. And about how Mike was trying to promote her into a management position for the new branch, but she didn't want to do it.

It had taken a while, but I finally realized that Mo and I both were at Bend High for a year. When I was a freshman, she was a senior. But back then she had real long, black hair and didn't have the tattoos or piercings. She looked totally different, which was probably why it had taken me so long to put it together.

I started sweeping the floor for the last time. I was humming along to the music but stopped suddenly, letting go of the broom.

The ghost boy was sitting at the last table, staring at me.

My heart thundered in my chest. It was time to figure out what he wanted.

I gathered up my courage and inched closer. I could see his scars clearly now, deep and dark across his face and arms. He had been in an accident, I was sure of that. A real bad accident.

I made my way over toward him. He was sitting on one of the chairs, his feet crossed in front of him. We looked at each other for a long time.

"Hey," I said, keeping my voice low. I didn't want Mo to hear me talking out loud, thinking I was insane.

"I'm Spenser," he finally said, nodding.

"Hi, Spenser," I said. "So how old are you?"

"Twelve," he said, looking around the coffee shop.

His dark hair was straight and thin, hanging past his shoulders. His pale skin bright against the shadows behind him.

I tried to seem relaxed so I wouldn't scare him away. But when I looked up at him again I saw that he was fading, disappearing before my eyes.

"Do you need my help with something?" I asked, feeling my knees buckle.

"I... I... messed up," he said softly.

"Messed up? What do you mean?" I asked.

He just nodded, and looked back up at me, his eyes urgent.

"Time is running out," he said.

I heard Mo come out from the back and he vanished, like he had never even been there.

"Okay, you almost done?" she shouted to me over the music. "Time to get outta here."

"Yeah," I said, taking off the apron, rubbing my arms to chase away the chills.

What did he mean I was running out of time?

At least I had a name. Spenser. It was a beginning.

We quickly finished boxing up the day-old muffins for the homeless shelter and left them on the counter for the pickup in the morning and grabbed our stuff and headed toward the door.

I turned abruptly to ask her if she had turned the lights off in the back when I caught sight of her arm and dropped my car keys on the floor.

"Oops," Mo said sarcastically.

But I just stood there, paralyzed, staring.

"Need help?" she said.

I nodded, but couldn't pry my eyes off the tattoo on her arm. I hadn't ever seen that one before.

It was a face.

It was Spenser.

## Chapter 14

I drove home in the dark, a combination of white flakes and rain falling steadily on the windshield, the wipers on high and the heat shooting out from all the vents.

As I headed down Bond, I was wishing that Jesse would just appear out of nowhere and be here next to me in the passenger's seat. I hadn't seen much of him lately and now, after seeing the ghost and seeing Mo's tattooed arm, I needed his help. I needed to talk to someone.

On the other hand, I knew he wouldn't want me to get involved with a ghost. The words were already on my tongue, but I held back from calling his name, from asking for help,

Maybe I could talk to Kate. It was time to tell her, anyway, that I was seeing a ghost. I promised her that I would always tell her about any ghosts, visions, or strange energies surrounding people. I didn't like to upset her, but I could see the importance of both of us knowing about those things.

I pulled up into the driveway and clicked the garage door opener. At night, we always parked our cars inside the garage now. It was a tight fit and as I drove in, I was careful not to scrape Kate's Subaru.

Kate opened the side door for me and I grabbed my bag and said hello as I walked into the house, the smell of fresh paint greeting me.

"Good day?" she asked.

"It was okay," I said. "How about you?"

"Yeah," she said. "Got it done."

We stood in the kitchen and I drank a glass of water. She told me about an interview she had with the forest service and the story she wrote. I told her about the chatty women who kept us working late and about how Mo finally kicked them out.

"Good for her," Kate said. "That's tough when that happens. Reminds me of when I worked at Red Robin back in high school. You still get paid, but it's not fun waiting around. I mean, just because someone's making minimum wage doesn't mean they don't have a life."

"Hey, I don't make minimum wage," I said.

I wasn't that far from it, but still.

"Stand down, Craig. No insult intended. I'm just saying, it's not like you and Mo own the place and you're making money off them. It's late. Get the hell out. What are they doing drinking coffee at ten at night anyway?"

"Who knows?" I said, yawning and rubbing my face.

"Hey, come look at the bathroom. I finished it tonight. Just about every room in the house has been painted. I just have the hallway and your room left and I'm done."

I followed the strong smell. She had done a nice job. The walls were darker than before, but looked fresh and clean.

"So it's green?" I asked.

"Yeah," she said. "Sage Green."

"Sounds nice," I said. "I mean, looks nice. Really nice. You've done a great job. The entire house looks, I don't know, elegant."

I yawned again.

"You want to get to bed? We can watch the show tomorrow night instead."

I had forgotten that we had made plans to see an episode of *Downton Abbey*. But I shook my head.

"No way. I want to see if Bates is charged with murder. Let me change and I'll be right out."

Kate and I had just discovered the British TV show about rich people and their servants. It sounded boring when she suggested it but had turned out to be a great series. We started watching it two weeks ago and were already deep into the second season.

I put on my pajamas, washed my face, and grabbed my new down comforter. I shuffled out to the living room and threw myself down on the slippery leather.

"You want any dinner?" she asked.

"No," I said. "Too late. I'm fine. I stuffed in a muffin at about eight."

"How about some tea? It would only take a minute."

"Nope, really I'm good."

"So how was the rest of your day?" she asked.

"Fine."

I sat trying to think of a way to tell her about the ghost, but was having trouble finding the words.

Kate paused the show and pulled her legs up, crossing them in front of her.

"So what's up?" she asked as she put down the remote.

I smiled. I had forgotten that it wasn't always so easy to hide things from her.

I spilled it. Everything. I didn't know if I was too tired or just desperate to tell someone, but I told Kate the entire story of seeing the ghost boy, out on the hiking trail, at the soccer park, and at work just a few hours ago. I made sure to emphasize that he didn't scare me, that he wasn't like

Annabelle. He wasn't angry or mean. He was just lost and needed some sort of help.

Her eyes narrowed and I could tell she was worried.

"Damn, Abby. I guess we should just be getting used to all this, but I wish they would leave you alone. But they don't. They keep trying to pull you back down into their crap."

There was anger in her voice. I finished telling her anyway, about Mo and her tattoo.

Kate sighed.

"Well, what can I do to help? You want me to try and research this kid, see if we can find out what happened to him?"

Kate was always Kate. My nose started stinging and I could feel the water pooling in my eyes as I thought about how lucky I was to have her in my life.

"Abby, you okay?" she said.

"I'm just tired," I said. "Let me see what Mo says. I work with her again soon. Maybe it won't be such a big deal. Maybe it's kind of like a translation gig, you know? The ghost boy just wants to tell her something."

Kate shifted in the sofa.

"Maybe it's her brother," she said.

"Yeah, that's what I was thinking. Thanks for listening. It helped."

"Good," she said, picking up the control. "Always tell me these things, Abby. We're in this together."

When she said that I almost lost it.

"Come on," I said. "Let's see what happens to Mister Bates."

"God, I hate that guy," Kate said as she started the show up.

"Me too," I said, the glow of the television bright in our faces.

## Chapter 15

I picked up a pair of socks and wandered around Dick's, checking out the Messi poster that was hanging above a display of jerseys. I had the same exact one in my room and had been looking for another, maybe one with the entire team, but they didn't have any. I would have to find it online.

It was an exciting time to be a Barcelona fan. They were looking strong as they headed into the quarterfinals of the Champions League. They also had a shot of winning *La Liga*, beating out their hated rivals, Real Madrid. And Messi looked as if he was a real contender for the *Pichichi*, the award given to the top scorer in the Spanish league.

"That guy knows soccer," a young guy said as he walked up to me.

"No one better," I said.

I was surprised actually that someone in the store even knew about Lionel Messi. While most agreed he was one of the greatest soccer players ever at only 24 years of age, and while millions of people around the world watched him play every week, most Americans had no idea who he was.

One of my dreams was to visit Spain someday and sit in the Camp Nou and watch my favorite team play a game.

Messi, Iniesta, Carles Puyol, Xavi, Dani Alves. I wanted to watch Pep Guardiola, the best soccer coach in the world, coaching the best soccer team in the world.

But my current wage of ten dollars an hour plus a few tips wasn't going to get me there anytime soon. Although I had started saving a little from my paycheck every week, I was only up to $250 and my car registration was due next month.

I made my way to the check out. There was a man in front of me and as I waited I pulled out my phone and checked for messages.

Mike asked, again, if I could come in an hour early. I texted him back telling him I could. I knew I would be working with Mo and was planning on asking her about the boy who was tattooed on her arm.

I always liked buying new soccer gear, even if it was just socks. It reminded me of the days when I played for my high school and flew all over that field, winning the ball and scoring. I was happy that I was playing again, but it wasn't the same and sometimes it made me sad thinking that, save for the odd fantasy, my glory days were behind me. I could have been in college now if I hadn't had the accident, maybe on a full scholarship, maybe even trying out for the US team.

But whenever it got me down, I told myself that anything could have happened. Nothing was a sure thing. Like what happened with Amanda, my ex-friend who I used to play with. She was starting goalie last year at a California college but then blew out her knee.

The cashier looked at me as I handed him my stuff, like he was waiting for something.

"Come on, Abby," he said, laughing. "Take a good look at my face."

It took me a moment to realize who it was.

"Conner?" I said. "Wow, it's really been a long time."

He came out from behind the register and gave me a hug before going back to ring up my things.

"So, you're back playing soccer," he said. "That's good, Abby. I'm glad."

I smiled, not really sure what to say. The last time I had talked to him he told me he was breaking up with me so he could date a cheerleader.

"It's been forever," he said, a little nervous. "Like we live in different cities or something. How have you been?"

He flipped back his hair like he always used to do when we were dating in high school. It felt like a lifetime ago. It was strange not seeing him for all these years. But that's how things were around here sometimes.

"Fine," I said. "How about you? What are you up to these days?"

"Just working and going to school part time. I've been here at Dick's for about a year. You know, the economy. But I'm taking classes over at the community college and I'll be transferring to U of O next year."

"That's great," I said.

"And you?" he asked, putting my stuff into a plastic bag.

I was quiet as I slid my debit card through the machine and punched in my pin number, thinking of something to say. I looked behind me, hoping a customer would come up, but the store was pretty empty.

"I work over at Back Street Coffee for now. Still trying to figure out the next move, I guess."

He nodded, his hair falling into his eyes and making him blink.

"Well, it was nice seeing you," I said, grabbing the bag and taking a few steps.

"Yeah," he said. "Hey, Abby, wait."

I stopped and turned back around facing him.

"Do you think we could meet up sometime? I mean, just as friends. For coffee or a beer. You know. I always felt bad about how we ended."

*You should*, I thought. Conner had acted like a total loser, the way he broke up with me, and at the time it broke my heart. But now, looking at him, that all seemed so long ago and unimportant. It was almost like it hadn't even happened.

"We'll see," I said.

I walked out of the store. As I put my bag in the back of the Jeep, I realized that Conner had actually helped me without even knowing it. When we were dating back in high school, I thought that I was in love with him. But after loving Jesse, I knew that it wasn't even close. And if Conner hadn't broken up with me, I might never have had that time with Jesse before the accident.

Really, it had worked out.

I headed to Back Street. Tonight was the night that I would tell Mo that there was a ghost who wanted to talk to her.

## Chapter 16

It was dead at Back Street from seven o'clock on and we were already talking about closing early. David left at eight, although he lingered for a while, practicing some of his lines in front of me. But when he got a phone call, he took off.

"Bye, you two," he said. "And remember, stop talking so much and get to work."

The bells on the door chimed after he left and I stood by the window, watching his Camaro tear out of the lot.

I took a deep breath. It wasn't something I was looking forward to, but I glanced back down at the table where the ghost was the other night and knew that I didn't have a choice.

"Hey, Mo," I said, walking up to her.

My voice was too high and I was nervous but I hoped she hadn't noticed. She was cleaning out one of the machines.

"Yeah?" she said, not looking up.

I thought about waiting to talk to her until we officially closed up because I didn't want to be interrupted if a customer came in. But it had been really quiet tonight.

"I need to talk to you," I said. She still didn't look at me. "About something important. Could we close up a few minutes early and talk then?"

She looked up finally, her dark eyes curious.

"Yeah, sure," she said slowly. "What about?"

Her energy darkened a little and I could tell she was annoyed. I couldn't blame her. She had no idea what it was about and being that we spoke exactly three sentences to each other all month, she was rightfully suspicious. Maybe she thought I was going to try and convert her, get her to join a church or something.

"It's about your tattoos. I just had a question."

"Go ahead," she said.

She put down the sponge and turned, facing me.

Our eyes met but I quickly looked away. I had a plan, knew what I wanted to say, but she wasn't making it easy and the words were all jumbled in my mind.

"Well…"

"So you're thinking of getting one after all," she interrupted. "I get them done in Eugene. I can give you the name of the guy if you want."

I shook my head.

"No, it's not that," I said, trying to smile and lighten the mood. "I'm too much of a chicken. No, I wanted to know about that one."

I pointed to her arm, and she held it out in front of her, trying to figure out the one I was talking about.

"This one?" she asked, touching the broken heart.

"No," I said.

She hesitated as she moved her finger down, touching his face. She didn't say anything.

"Yeah. That one."

As she glanced at her arm, I could see that I had hit a raw nerve and could almost hear the pain inside her in the silence that followed.

83

"What about it?" she said finally.

"Well, I was just wondering who that was."

She looked over at the door as if a customer had come in, but nobody was there. When she looked back at me, her eyes were flat. She sighed loudly.

I played with the towel I was holding. The conversation wasn't going as I had hoped, but there was nothing else to do. The ghost boy was connected to her and I had to find out about him so he would leave me alone.

"Spenser. He was my brother," she said. "He died in an accident."

I nodded.

"I'm sorry," I said. "Thanks for telling me."

She studied me for a moment, and then started walking away.

"Wait," I said.

She turned around and came up to me, a little too close.

"Look, I get asked about this once in a while. I get it. It's a tattoo and some people think I'm putting it out there for the world to see and for them to ask me about it. They think I want to talk about it to them. But they're full of shit. That's not why it's on my arm."

"That's not where I'm coming from," I said.

And then I dropped it on her. All of it.

"I see ghosts sometimes and I've seen him. I've seen Spenser."

She didn't move, didn't even blink. And for a moment I had the feeling she might slap my face or throw a punch into my gut, but she didn't. She just stared at me for a long time before heading into the back of the store.

I knew exactly how she felt. I didn't like to talk about these kinds of things either. But I was going to have to. I didn't follow her. I flipped the sign and closed the blinds and sat down at the table and waited.

Mo came back out a few minutes later and saw me sitting.

"Come on, we got work to do," she said, shouting over the music.

"One more thing, Mo," I said.

She came over. She folded her arms and stopped a few feet away, still glaring at me. I held her chilling look, and then saw the resemblance. She had the same serious eyes as Spenser.

"I know you don't know me that well, but I bet you know a little bit about me. I bet you've heard some of the stories," I said.

I was taking a shot, but it was a good one. I could tell by the expression on her face that she had heard about me. For a while after my drowning, I was known all over town as the girl who came back from the dead. It felt like everyone knew my story. I would be in a store and strangers would come up and talk to me like they knew me. Some of them were scared of me. Some of them thought I was cursed.

And being that Mo and I had gone to the same high school, she probably would have been familiar with my name. There was also a good chance that she had heard about me dying and then coming back to life.

But she still didn't say anything.

"Your brother…" I started, but she wouldn't let me finish.

"Stop it," she said, holding up her hand. "I don't know what scam you're working, but I'm not buying it. Just leave me alone. Back the fuck away, Love Hewitt."

Her voice was shaky and sharp.

"He says he needs help. But I don't know how to help him without knowing more about him. He's following me around. He was even here, over in that corner the other night."

She turned around and looked at the table I was point-ing to.

"He wears a Guns N' Roses T-shirt and jeans and has scars and bruises all over his face. I'm just trying to help him, Mo. But I need more information about him."

She walked over to a table and picked up a balled-up napkin and stuffed it in the trashcan.

"You seem all buddy-buddy with my dead brother," she said. "Just ask *him* and leave me the hell out of it."

She walked back over to the machines and finished cleaning them out. We didn't speak the rest of the night.

# Chapter 17

As I took a batch of lemon cookies out of the oven, I couldn't stop thinking about Mo. Asking about her brother and then telling her that I had seen his ghost lurking around the coffee shop had been a mistake. We had worked together two times since that night, and she still wasn't talking to me, even though I had gone out of my way to be friendly. She was still angry, her energy dark.

But I couldn't just drop it. I needed a new plan.

The cookies were for Ty, who was on his way over. We were going out to dinner and a movie.

I let them cool on the rack, and then ate one before sliding some into a tin. It was the first time I had used the recipe and they were sweet and tart at the same time.

Kate was in the hallway, up on a ladder.

"I left you some cookies under the glass dome," I said, standing under her.

"Thanks," she said, gliding a paintbrush across the wall, right under the ceiling. "They smell like hazelnut."

"What color is it?" I asked, thinking it odd because I hadn't used hazelnuts.

"Hazelnut," she said.

"Sounds like a good one."

She glanced down at me.

"You look nice. When is Ty picking you up?"

"He should be here any minute," I said. "Are you sure you don't want to come with us?"

"No, but thanks. I want to finish."

I was happy that Kate was almost done with all the painting, although I wasn't sure what she would do now with her extra time. I was really looking forward to not smelling those strong paint fumes every time I came home and opened the door.

"All right," I said. "Oh, I forgot to tell you that I bumped into Conner the other day."

"Conner? Oh, yeah. You mean that worthless punk you dated in high school?"

"Yeah. I was buying some new soccer socks and as I was checking out, there he was. He works at Dick's."

Kate stopped painting.

"How apropos," she said, smiling. "Being that he is one."

I heard a noise out front. I went to the living room and saw Ty outside in the driveway. He grabbed something from the bed of his truck. When I opened the door, he was coming up the path, carrying two of the old coffee cans we had found in the desert, each one full of daffodils.

He handed me one and gave me a quick kiss. I had those usual fluttery feelings that flew around inside whenever I saw him.

"Wow, this really does look cool," I said, staring down at the can. "Thanks."

He greeted Kate and handed her the flowers and told her the story about how we had found hundreds of burned out cans in a pile when we were hiking in the Badlands.

"I thought it looked kind of Western and artsy," he said. "Perfect for the lodge theme you have going on here."

I was surprised how she really seemed to love the can and flowers as much as he did. She put hers on one of the new tables.

"They're fantastic," she said. "You really have an artist's eye."

It made me happy that they were such good friends. It felt right.

"Kate, come with us," he said, when he heard she was staying home. "Or how about meeting us at the movie later?"

"No, I'm going to pass. But you guys have a great evening."

"Okay," he said. "But if you change your mind, we're going to the 10 o'clock showing of the new Liam Neeson movie."

"I'll keep that in mind," she said. "But honestly, I'll be in bed by then with my Kindle."

She gave him a kiss on the cheek.

"Bye, guys," she said.

"Bye," I said.

I grabbed my new Guess jacket off the coat rack and put it on and then remembered the cookies and headed back to the kitchen.

"These are for you," I said.

"Excellent," Ty said, taking the tin from my hands. He opened it up and inhaled deeply and then took a cookie and stuffed it in his mouth.

"Amazing," he said. "Thanks, Abby."

As we drove over to the Old Mill, we talked about work and the things that happened over the last few days. It was always good to see Ty and I noticed that the energy that surrounded him was bright and moving fast as we talked.

He kept his window opened a crack, even though it was freezing outside, and his light, long hair blew around in the air. Ty was never cold. Sometimes he picked me up in shorts and a hoodie when it was snowing.

"How was work?' I asked.

"Good. I'm still hoping that they'll teach me how to brew."

"Do you like 10 Barrel beer as much as the beer at Deschutes?"

I remembered Ty's story about how Deschutes Brewery was the reason he moved here from Montana.

"I do," he said. "Deschutes is good, but there are a lot of really great beers here in Bend. 10 Barrel knows their stuff. And I have to say I'm looking forward to learning how to brew. I could totally get into that."

I flipped on the radio and found the new rock station. Sometimes Mike put it on at work and so far I liked it. As we cruised down 14th, a song from one of the local bands I had heard at work came on.

We decided to go to Flatbread Pizza. We went there once in a while, when I could drag Ty away from the pubs.

"You look great, by the way," he said, putting his arm around my shoulders as we walked slowly past the movie theater, past REI, and toward the restaurants.

We got a booth and ordered. After the waitress left, Ty finished telling me about his day at work and I told him about Mike being okay with the river job in the summer.

"So, did Brad get hired as a guide?" I asked.

"They're still thinking about it," he said, picking up a breadstick. "I don't know. Now Rebecca is saying that they might not hire anybody new this summer and just let us absorb the extra hours."

"I hope they change their mind," I said, now that I had told Mike I wanted to work both jobs. Last summer, Ty was working seven days a week on the river.

I tried to think of things to tell him about my week. I wished that I could tell him about all the things that were happening, like how I saw the ghost or about how Mo was mad at me. Ty was great with people and if I told him, he could probably offer some good suggestions on how to talk to her.

It couldn't be good for a relationship to have such secrets, but I didn't want him to think he was dating someone who rented headspace out to squirrels. Plus, I wasn't really sure what Ty's reaction would be if I was honest and told him I saw ghosts. Some things can't be predicted.

And that I talked with Jesse once in a while.

Ty and I had never discussed religion or beliefs or any of that stuff. The only thing I was sure of was that he hated all those popular vampire movies. I knew if we were to continue and if things were going to get serious between us, I would have to tell him. Eventually.

But not tonight.

"What do you want to do for your birthday?" he asked.

"Come on. You sound like my sister," I said. "It's still months away."

"It's not that far away. And it's the big one. How 'bout we go bar hopping?"

"Okay, let me think on that," I said.

"You'll like it," Ty said. "You'll see."

I took a bite of the pizza.

"Don't let Kate throw me a party. She's been hinting at it and it would be great if you could tell her that I'm not up for it. I don't want to hurt her feelings, but I really don't want one."

"Okay," he said. "I'll let her know. So what then?"

"I'll give it some thought. Something quiet. But special."

It was funny talking like this with Ty, discussing these plans for the future. It was nice, comfortable.

I argued with him when the bill came, but he insisted on handing his credit card to the waitress and then went to the restroom.

The tingling feeling that bubbled up inside when I was with him felt nice. But sometimes it made me feel like I was betraying Jesse.

We still had a little time before the movie so we strolled along the river, holding hands, up and over the bridge where plastic flags flapped wildly in the bitter wind. The clouds were gone and it was a moonless sky with thousands of brilliant stars scattered in the blackness above.

I tilted my head all the way back, breathing in the night.

# Chapter 18

The howl of the train whistle in my ears was deafening.

I fell into the cold, dark water and sank down, down, down past the bubbles that were rising up all around me. I tried to reach for the surface, tried to get to the air but couldn't. It kept getting farther and farther away. I was being pulled down to the bottom and I couldn't hold my breath for much longer.

But suddenly, I was out of the water, breathing again, down in an even deeper darkness, the train still loud in my ears.

I didn't know where I was. I was walking in the dark, my bare feet on the cold ground. Fear surged through me. There was a faint glow up ahead and I moved slowly toward it, one foot in front of the other.

I came to a door and pushed against it, but it wouldn't open more than a few inches. It was bright in there, but I couldn't see much. It was a room, with furniture and a long table pushed up against the wall. A television was on in the background and I could hear the sound of drums.

Someone was there. A shadow moved past the open crack as I looked inside.

I tried again to open the door, but it wouldn't budge. The shadow swayed and danced across the room. I couldn't see who it was, couldn't make out a face. Suddenly a strong smell, a chemical of some sort, filled my nostrils and then smoke started filling the room. It was hard to breathe.

I backed away, away from the light, and then I was suddenly swimming. Up, up, up to the surface, leaving the shadow figure far behind, buried somewhere at the bottom of the lake. I moved my arms through the water in hard, furious strokes, faster and faster, finally breaking the surface just before my lungs exploded.

And then I started screaming, the train still howling.

\*\*\*

"Abby!" Kate said, shaking me. "Abby. Wake up. You're having a nightmare."

I sat up. My heart pounded and tears streamed down my cheeks.

"It's okay," she said over and over again until I finally heard it.

Until I believed it.

She wrapped both arms around me and held me for a long time, stroking my hair.

"You're safe, Abby. You're here at home. I'm here with you. Nobody is going to hurt you."

I ran to the bathroom, feeling like I was going to throw up. Kate followed me and rubbed my back as I leaned over the toilet. Staring down at the water just made it worse and I backed away, managing to hold it down. I washed my face and sobbed and she handed me a towel. She helped me put on my robe and slippers.

She led me to the living room and wrapped a fleece blanket around me and we sat in the dark stillness, not saying anything. I stared at the light outside that was filtering through the curtains. She put her arm over my shoulders.

"You're okay, Abby," she kept repeating. "You're okay."

I didn't feel okay. I felt dark and terrible, but I nodded anyway.

"It's over. It was just a dream. A nightmare."

But I knew that wasn't true. It was something more.

"Do you want to talk about it?"

I shook my head.

"How about some tea?"

"Okay," I said.

She got up and I heard her banging around in the kitchen. It seemed like she was gone for only a minute and she returned carrying two mugs.

She put the cup in my hands and I blew on the steam.

"Thanks."

"What was it about?"

"I don't even know. Darkness. Shadows. But Kate, it wasn't a nightmare."

She put her mug down on the table and looked at me.

"What do you mean?"

I glanced up at her, studying her face. She knew what I meant.

"It was one of those visions, when I'm in the lake and then I'm thrown out and I see people or something. It was one of those."

"Like after your accident? When you had those visions about him killing people here in Bend?"

I nodded.

She sat back, her eyes wide.

"Damn," she said. "Did you see him?"

"No, I didn't see him. But I think he was there, Kate. I think he was watching someone. He was watching this guy walking around. It had a bad feeling. Just like those visions. Just like when he killed all those people."

"Abby, it's impossible. He's dead. He's not able to kill people anymore. You saw his body. Ben buried him. There's just no way."

I knew what she was saying was true. I drank the tea in uneven gulps. I think I knew now what people meant when they said they could really use a drink.

# Chapter 19

We spent the entire night talking about dreams and visions and Nathaniel Mortimer. When dawn finally crept in, I told Kate I would call and make an appointment to see Dr. Krowe.

"Good," she said. "And let him give you something so you can get some sleep."

"All right," I said, fighting off a yawn.

I was hoping what she said was true too, that it was just a dream and not one of those visions I used to have. But it sure had felt the same. Starting off in that dark lake, drowning. It had felt the same, although I had trouble explaining that to Kate.

Not long after my drowning accident, I had a series of visions in which I witnessed Nathaniel Mortimer stalk and kill four people. Following the murders he had injected each of the victims with his serum. At the time I didn't know that he was killing them so he could bring them back to life. It didn't work.

In the last vision, Nathaniel had seen me watching him and even smiled at me. He told me later that we had a special bond. And now I was terrified that my greatest fear was coming true. That death wouldn't be able to keep us apart.

I never understood the visions. Why I had them, or why they stopped. I was just grateful that they had.

But regardless, Kate was right about one thing.

It was time to see Dr. Krowe.

## Chapter 20

I was surprised that Dr. Krowe could see me so fast and that he had an opening that afternoon. I would have to go into work an hour later, so I called Mike to make sure it was okay.

"Sure," he said. "Lyle can probably cover it. You okay?"

"Oh, yeah," I said. "It's just a dentist appointment I forgot about."

"Oh, well good then. See you at three," he said.

I called Kate at work to let her know. She sounded tired, but perked up when I told her about the appointment.

"Say hi for me," she said.

It still felt like going backwards, especially on the drive over, but I didn't think too much about it. My sleep-deprived brain didn't seem up to the task. I focused instead on stop lights, pedestrians, and safe lane changes. As I pulled in and parked by the small wood building tucked away next to some trees, all sorts of feelings sprouted up, making me want to cry.

I remembered those times I came here, believing all the while that Jesse was still alive, when everyone knew the truth. He had died in the accident.

But Dr. Krowe had helped me once, and had helped me a lot. I had told him everything in the end, about the visions, about seeing Jesse's ghost. Everything. And he believed me. He was cool that way, willing to be open to the fact that there were paranormal events in the world that couldn't easily be explained.

Really, he was one of the good guys.

So maybe it wasn't that bad seeing him again. It was kind of like visiting an old friend. That's how I was going to look at it anyway.

I knocked on the door.

"Abby," he said, his face lighting up. "It is so good to see you."

He gave me a hug, which surprised me.

"Hey, Dr. Krowe. How are you doing?"

"Good, good. Come on in."

The door closed behind me as I stepped into his office. It felt like I had never left.

"Please, sit down."

I did and glanced around the office. Everything was exactly the same. The leather chairs, the paintings on the walls, the immaculate desk. The ceramic elephant paperweight that one of his kids must have made for him.

I hadn't seen Dr. Krowe in a while. But he looked the same. And when he sat down with his pen and pad of paper, I saw that he was still a fan of those argyle socks he always used to wear. From the smell his clothes gave off, I could also tell that he was still smoking.

"I'm glad you decided to come in and see me," he said. "I talk to Kate sometimes and she told me about some of the things that have been going on."

A tiny spark of anger went off somewhere inside me, but it was like trying to start a fire with wet kindling. I was too tired. I wasn't going to hold it against her, I decided. Kate doing her best David impersonation, flapping her gums around town. I knew she had my best interest at heart.

His eyes were friendly but heavy.

"It's nice seeing you, Dr. Krowe," I said. "But I have to be honest. I'm not sure I belong here. It feels like, I don't know, like I'm going backwards a little. I don't like that feeling."

It was a rehearsed line, and sounded that way. But I wanted to open with it. He always told me to express my feelings, so I figured I should.

"That makes perfect sense. But you're not really going backwards, Abby. Most of my patients come and go and then come back again. It's very common. It's just, well, life."

That made sense to me.

"So, what should we talk about today? You could start with what you've been doing these past few years if you'd like."

His pen moved across the paper as I told him about being a river guide, playing soccer, and working at Back Street. None of it sounded that exciting, but he seemed happy as he wrote it all down.

"Wow. Abby, I congratulate you. You've really built a great life, haven't you? That's outstanding. And I can't believe you were a river guide last summer, going back out on the water after your accident."

"Yeah. It felt good being out there. I'm doing it again, too. I start in June."

"That's just amazing. Does it scare you, being so close to the water like that after you drowned?"

I liked how he just came out with it. *After you drowned.* No trace of hesitation in his voice. He wasn't walking on eggshells around me. He was treating me like I was all right. Maybe he was giving me more credit than I deserved. Lately anyway.

"Sure," I said. "I think the rapids scare everyone. They should anyway."

He nodded.

"How did Kate feel about you being a river guide?"

I shrugged.

"She accepted it. But it wasn't easy. I haven't told her that I've already signed my contract for this year. She worries, you know."

But I was thinking, really, it was the least of our worries. He nodded and wrote down some things and uncrossed his legs.

"Speaking of Kate, she told me about the kidnapping. I'm wondering if you're comfortable talking about that."

I glanced out at the trees, something dark simmering inside, and nodded slowly.

"So this Nathaniel Mortimer, Dr. Ben Mortimer's brother, he claims, I'm sorry, claimed. I see now that he is deceased. Nathaniel claimed that he was the one who saved you. That he brought you back from the dead. He told you that he was the reason you survived your drowning accident? Did I understand all that right?"

I nodded again.

"And then he kidnapped you to perform tests?"

I nodded again, holding my hands together and hoping he wouldn't notice how I had started shaking.

"Abby, it's no wonder you're not sleeping. We don't have to start discussing this in our first session. I just wanted to make sure I knew all the facts, that I understood what had happened. But we can take as long as you need to sort all this out. You've been through a difficult trauma and I'm so glad you've decided to come see me. That shows me that you're taking care of yourself."

Apparently Kate had told him everything.

"Do you have trouble every night?" he asked.

"Yeah."

"Nightmares?"

"Yeah."

The pen squeaked as he wrote it down.

"For how long?"

"Since I got back. Five months."

"So you haven't really had a good night's sleep in five months?"

I thought about it for a moment.

"I had a week or so that was good. In February."

"But that's it?"

"That's it."

He nodded and waited for me to look at him.

"You have to sleep, Abby," he said. "It's important. Really important. I think it's a good starting place."

"I know. I guess that's one of the reasons why I'm here."

He wrote something else down and then got up and went over to his desk. He brought back a small pad and scribbled on it.

"Here's a prescription," he said. "One pill right before bed and you'll start sleeping through the night."

I reached over and took the paper, folding it and putting it in my pocket.

"Thanks."

I wasn't sure yet if I was going to take them. I needed to think it over.

"Just so you know, I don't usually prescribe sleeping pills, but in your case I think it's a good idea, just for a little while. I've given you enough for a week. Let's reassess after that."

"Okay."

"Good."

I stayed the entire hour, filling it with a few stories about the people at Back Street, my running program, signing up for soccer again through Parks and Rec. The easy stuff.

Next time, we would take it a step forward. Next time, I would tell him all about Nathaniel and what he did to me.

# Chapter 21

Mo still wasn't speaking to me.

It had been over a week and we had worked together a few times, but clearly she was holding a grudge. She hadn't said one word to me.

I hadn't seen Spenser again and hadn't learned anything new. There was nothing to do but wait. I went about my life, working at the coffee house, practicing my moves and shots at the park, hanging out with Ty.

The pills sat untouched on my nightstand. I thought about taking them every night, but so far I hadn't even opened the bottle. I still equated them with a complete loss of control, with Nathaniel and the drugs he had given me during the kidnapping. I never wanted to feel that way again.

"Why don't you take one and then sleep with me in my bed?" Kate had suggested. We were at Home Depot late one night, looking at floor tiles.

"Yeah, that sounds good."

She waited, then finished my thought.

"But not tonight, right?"

"No, not tonight."

It was bothering me that I hadn't seen Spenser in all this time. I got the idea that maybe he had figured out that

Mo didn't want to talk to him and he'd moved on. There were probably things he wanted to tell her. But maybe he saw his sister's intense energy darken when I tried to talk to her about him.

But the ghost boy's sad eyes stayed with me, and so did his words. He told me that he messed up and I wanted to know what that meant. In the early morning hours before dawn, when I lay in bed thinking about everything, my thoughts turned back to him.

And what kind of help did he need?

When I got up in the morning, I decided to take one last shot at finding out more about Spenser. And I had a good idea who might be able to help.

***

"So, how about grabbing a drink after work later?" I asked David as I stacked white mugs in a neat row under the counter.

The timing was perfect. We were both off in the afternoon.

"Abby Craig! You surprise me every day," he said. "I would love to. What time were you thinking?"

"Well, how about we meet up at three," I said.

I helped the woman who walked up carrying a small dog. We didn't allow dogs inside, but I rang up her order and waited before pointing it out, just to see if she was staying. She took her latte and went outside.

"Yeah. Sounds fun," he said. "Where do you want to go?"

"Wherever you want. Deschutes. 10 Barrel. McMenamins."

"Let's go to 10 Barrel," he said. "We'll say hello to BB."

I smiled.

"He's not on until later."

"Let's go anyway. They have great brews on tap and you can sneak some sips from my glass when nobody's looking."

I was glad that Ty wouldn't be working then. I didn't want David to talk about my beautiful boyfriend all afternoon. I wanted to have a serious conversation.

I wanted him to tell me everything he knew about Mo.

# Chapter 22

I was all ready to sit outside, but David refused, saying it was way too cold still.

"You're kidding! Right?"

It had been a beautiful day, with temperatures in the high 60s and only a few clouds.

"Sorry. That little wind in the afternoon is a real killer."

"All right. All right, you baby."

We walked inside, taking a seat at a table next to the window.

I stopped by 10 Barrel once in a while when Ty was working. They had good food and I liked the atmosphere. But I wasn't so hungry now so I just ordered a Coke.

David clasped his hands together on the table and leaned forward.

"So, Abby Craig, tell me what you want to talk about."

I smiled. David was a smart guy. He reminded me of Kate sometimes, being able to read people's emotions and always knowing when a customer was anxious or mad. I didn't bother with insisting that I had invited him out just for fun and small talk.

"Mo," I said.

"Yeah, no kidding. What's with you two? Feels like the North Pole when I'm around you guys. What happened?"

I didn't want to tell David everything, just enough to get him to help me.

"I asked about one of her tattoos and she freaked out."

He nodded.

"You asked about Spenser, right?" he said.

"Yeah," I said, playing it up a little. "Big mistake."

"No, Abby Craig. You were just being inquisitive. Don't beat yourself up that way. I did the same thing when I started working there and the next minute I thought I was a gazelle at a Serengeti watering hole, taking my last sip of water before a lion had me for breakfast. *Watch out says that bird*, if you know what I mean."

The waiter brought out our drinks and David took a sip of his beer.

"She's just a very sensitive girl. And most people don't realize that. It's hard to tell, but she's hiding a lot of pain behind all that makeup and fuchsia hair."

I laughed.

"What's so funny?" he said.

"I didn't know she had fuchsia hair. I thought it was brown or something."

"Oh, yeah," he said. "I am always forgetting about your color blindness thing. She changes her hair color like every other week. But just up front here."

He moved his hands around his head.

"Sometimes it's pink, sometimes green. I'm a natural dirty blonde, in case you were wondering."

He ran his fingers through his hair, showing me.

"So what? Does it look like I have white hair to you?"

"Kind of a salt and pepper look."

"Eeww," David said. "That's such a bummer, Abby Craig, not seeing colors. Have you always been that way?"

I shook my head.

"No," I said cautiously. I didn't want to get into my story. "I can remember what most colors look like. But someone has to say what they are and then I'll try to visualize them."

I told him about Kate and how she was painting the house and how she always was telling me what the colors were but how they were pretty much all shades of gray to me.

"Yuck," he said. "Can't they do something for that? It's like the 21st century. They can do anything."

I shrugged as I sat back in the seat.

"Maybe someday," I said. "Hopefully."

The waiter stopped by our table and asked how everything was and David started talking to him about how he had to wait two hours one time back in the summer to get a table with his friends outside. When the waiter left, he started talking about the different people who worked at Back Street over the last year. I tried to think about how to get our conversation back on track.

"David Norton," I said, interrupting him. "I need your help."

That seemed to do the trick.

"Tell me what you need," he said, his face serious.

"How did Spenser die?"

He looked around, as if checking to make sure Mo wasn't sitting behind us. The tables were filling up, but she wasn't there.

"He was killed by a hit and run driver one night out on China Hat Road. They found his body by the side of the road in the morning. Sad, huh? It was a while ago, like three years. Spenser was a lot younger than Mo, but I'm guessing they were really tight."

"So it was an accident," I said.

"Yep. The woman who hit him turned herself in the next day. She did a little time for it. Get this. She was talking on her cell phone at the time and said that Spenser just ran out in front of her. But Mo said she doesn't believe the bitch. She says that she must have swerved into him as she was gabbing and didn't pay attention."

A heaviness hung over us as I thought about what Mo had gone through.

I glanced around. There were a lot more people now and they all seemed so happy, laughing and drinking, meeting up with friends. I wondered why some people were so lucky, while others weren't.

"I'm surprised she talks to you about it," I said. "She was very clear that she didn't like to talk about Spenser at all."

"Well, I have a little trick with that," David said. "Alcohol. She only talks about things like that when she's hammered. You know, I see her out at the bars a lot. We hang together sometimes."

He sighed, played with the paper wrapping from my straw.

"But I promised her that I wouldn't ever say anything about this. And now look at me. Big Mouth Jones. It's your fault. You've filled me with beer and I've spilled my guts."

"I thought your last name was Norton."

"Norton. Jones. What's in a name?"

He was kind of kidding, but I could see that he also felt bad. He drained his glass.

"Well, this is all on me," I said.

"Damn right it is, girlfriend," he said, pouting. "And by the way, I'm not cheap."

He signaled the waiter and ordered another beer and some French fries.

"I appreciate it, David. Really. Thanks."

"Look. Just leave her alone and she'll come around and eventually return to the six words a day she used to say to you. That's my best advice. Just don't mention Spenser again."

I smiled.

The young waiter came back with the food and David told him about how I was dating Ty.

"I know Ty," the waiter said, smiling. "You must be Abby."

"Yeah," I said.

"I'm John. He talks about you all the time. Good to meet you."

I smiled shyly, not knowing what to say. He left and I rolled my eyes at David.

"What? Everybody in the place needs to know that BB is off limits," he said. "There's too many cute young things working here. I'm just looking out for you, Abby Craig."

I couldn't help but laugh and I was glad the mood of our conversation had lightened up. And then I made a decision.

"You see," I said.

It was an awkward start, but David was listening.

"Well, I see ghosts sometimes. And I've seen Spenser and I'm just trying to help him."

I couldn't look at David as I spoke, resting my eyes instead on the dog tied up outside to a chair. When I glanced back, he had a huge grin on his face and his energy danced around him.

"That's fantastic. But for reals? You're serious? You're like that girl on that TV show who wears those wigs and false eyelashes? I love her! Have you seen her new series?"

"No. Yeah. It's true. I see ghosts."

"Wow," he said. "Just wow."

112

He leaned back and ate some of the fries, moving the plate over between us. I took a few.

"So you think he wants to tell her something? Like the winning numbers for the Lotto?"

"I don't know. But it's something serious. I don't know what it is. Maybe there's more to how he died and he's trying to tell Mo. He's sad. And lost."

"Oh, my God. Maybe something's going to happen to Mo. Is it your experience that ghosts come back to warn people?"

I shrugged. I didn't really have that much experience with ghosts. Just three. And they were all so different.

"I've only talked to a few of them. Maybe he just wants to say he's sorry for something. Or that he misses her. If they were close, it's probably something like that. That's my guess, but I'm not really sure."

Kings of Leon poured out through the speakers. It was getting crowded. I looked at my watch. It was already close to four.

"I couldn't agree more," David said, listening to the music as he eyed John from behind. "I wonder if these guys were thinking of a delicious little waiter when they wrote this song. Probably not, huh?"

"David, please try to focus here. The bottom line is that I need Mo to listen to what I have to say. Spenser is around me because of her. And he keeps popping up."

"Scary."

"It is scary."

I told him about how Spenser showed up in the goal box when I was practicing soccer.

"That doesn't surprise me. He was a player on one of those club teams. The family was really involved in all that. Like, traveling all weekend, going to California and Idaho for tournaments. That's what Mo told me once anyway."

"One more thing," I said. "I know this is probably asking for the moon, but I hope you can plug that hole you have in your gut just this once. I really don't need this getting out all over town, you know, that I see ghosts."

"For you, Abby Craig, I'll stick a cork in it where the sun don't shine."

"Too much information, David. Way too much information."

# Chapter 23

Kate was in the kitchen making dinner and I brought out my computer and sat in the living room googling Spenser McSorley to see what I could find out. When I saw all the stories on his accident, I kicked myself for not doing it sooner.

There wasn't really too much beyond what David had told me, but there were a lot of articles covering the basics. Straight forward crime accounts about how a student from High Desert Middle School had been killed in a hit-and-run accident. I also found some photos. It was nice seeing Spenser without scars and smiling. I found his sixth grade school portrait, pictures of him with his soccer team, and shots of him with his family that showed Mo as I had remembered her from high school.

Spenser McSorley seemed like a happy kid, posing for the camera like he had his entire life in front of him.

I wondered if he had had Olympic soccer dreams too. He was a good athlete. He played goalkeeper on a club team that had gone on to win the State Championship. It didn't surprise me. I could tell he knew his stuff that day when we played together on the field. Even though his ghostly hands now put him at a decided disadvantage.

Judy Elgin had confessed to hitting Spenser on a foggy night in March at about 10 p.m. She pleaded guilty to manslaughter, admitting that she was on her cell phone at the time but insisting that it wasn't the cause of the accident. She said that Spenser darted out in front of her suddenly, running out from an open field onto the quiet road.

She was given an 18-month sentence but was released after serving three.

"Dinner is ready," Kate said.

I walked over to the kitchen and helped bring out the plates and silverware. It was simple, a roasted chicken and a salad, but it hit the spot.

Later I filled her in on what I had found out. I told her as we opened up boxes of ceramic tile that had been stacked in the corner next to the door.

"Now I remember," she said. "It was such a terrible story. It was only about a month or so after your accident. Kyle covered it and had to go out and interview the parents. It was heartbreaking. Poor Mo."

"Yeah."

"I wonder if Ben was working in the emergency room that night."

"Maybe, huh."

"Did you read Kyle's story?"

"No. I tried to get some of those stories off *The Bugler* website, but they wanted a credit card first."

"Yeah. Pretty stupid policy," Kate said. "We get a lot of complaints about the pay wall, but the editor refuses to lift it. Caveman thinking there. Maybe with the newspaper going bankrupt last year they need the money."

I laughed.

"Just let me know what you want and I'll get it for you from the online archives."

But I had what I needed and told her. Kate held up a tile and studied it.

"I love those," I said.

"Me, too. I've never put in tiles before. It should be interesting."

"Do you want some help? I was going to watch the *Monster Man* finale, but I could just record it."

"Not tonight. I wasn't going to start putting them in yet."

"Okay, just let me know," I said.

"So you have a day off tomorrow?" she asked.

"Yeah," I said.

"Promise me you won't go in, even if Mike calls. You've been working too much lately."

I had already decided to let the phone go to voicemail if he called, but it was nice that Kate suggested it.

"Promise."

"So, what are you going to do?" she asked.

"I'm not really sure. Soccer practice. Drop by the bank. Not too much beyond that, really."

She was quiet and I walked over to my computer and closed it.

"Abby, I want you to tell me the truth."

I stared at her for a minute, trying to figure out what she was talking about and where the conversation was headed.

"What do you mean?"

"Why aren't you taking those sleeping pills?"

"I don't know. They scare me a little, I guess."

"But do you ever sleep at night anymore? I hear you walking around all the time out here. And you look exhausted."

I looked at her, a little sheepishly.

"Sure I sleep."

She shook her head.

"No you don't."

"I take a lot of naps. And I sleep late in the mornings. I'm okay. Really."

"I think it's time to take them."

That was all. There was no long, drawn out discussion or insistence. But it was in the way she said it, her voice steeped in worry, full of dread. Like she saw something I couldn't.

Like she saw what was coming.

# Chapter 24

"I'm going to get some more beans from the back," David said to me in a low voice. "I'll be back in ten minutes or so."

That seemed like a crazy long time to fill a container, but we weren't that busy so I didn't care. Maybe David was going to take his break back there.

I was relieved that he hadn't called me a ghost whisperer or something like that when I came in to start my afternoon shift. Actually he had been really cool about my secret so far, not once acknowledging that I saw ghosts. He didn't even make any jokes about it when we were alone. I didn't know how long it was going to last, but I was hoping that me telling David would pay off in the end and that I wouldn't get burned.

The afternoon hours flew by quickly and it was already almost seven. I was uneasy when I thought that after he left, Mo and I would be by ourselves. I caught her glancing my way a few times, but she still hadn't spoken to me. Maybe I would just have to get used to it.

I finished cleaning out the large brewer and then rang up a few orders. We said goodbye to David and I packed up all the used grounds, thinking about whether I should bring them home for Kate. She was planning on doing some serious gardening now that she was almost done painting the house.

Out of the corner of my eye, I saw Mo walking toward me.

"Let's talk after we close," she said.

"Sure, okay."

Her energy was more relaxed, not as dark, and calmer than it had been all week. I wondered if David had said something to her.

A new round of customers came in, got in line, and ordered. The next time I looked up at the clock it was almost time to go home. We started our cleaning routine, Mo counting the money. By 9:10, everybody was gone and we locked the doors.

She turned down Larry and his Flask, one of the local bands. She went over to a table by the window and waited. I finished putting away the milk, took off my apron, and sat down across from her.

"Tell me what you saw," she said, slouching back in the chair.

"I've seen your brother," I said. "Three times now. Once on a hike. Once at Big Sky Park. And then over there at that corner table like I told you. I think he wants to talk to you."

She pushed out the chair next to her and put her feet on it, but didn't say anything. I waited while we stewed in the uncomfortable silence.

"So did David talk to you?" I said, not being able to take it anymore.

"About what?"

"Me."

"Only that I should ease up on you. I don't know what business it is of his. Typical."

She sighed and I could see that it wasn't easy for her, talking to me. But we were making progress. I tried to think of something to say.

"I figured you wouldn't ever want to talk about this with me."

She sat up in the chair.

"So what changed your mind about listening to what I had to say?" I said.

"Well, he is my brother. Seems only right. Plus, what you said. About what he was wearing. The Guns N' Roses T-shirt."

"Yeah, he's had it on every time I've seen him."

"That band rocked his world. He used to do a pretty cool Axl impression."

She smiled briefly, but then it disappeared.

"And I don't know how you would know about his favorite rock band," she said. "I mean, that seems like proof. Although I guess you could have seen him way back when we were in high school. But I don't think so."

"I barely remember you, let alone your brother."

Even if Mo had been in my class, I doubted I would have known her that well. We traveled in different circles.

"I remember you. I saw you play once. You were all right."

"Thanks," I said, a little surprised.

"And you were right about that other thing you said too. I do remember your accident. It was right before Spenser's. When you started working here, I knew who you were."

I leaned in toward her.

"Mo, can you tell me about that night? It might help."

She looked off and we hit another few minutes of dead air. But I was patient and didn't rush her. I knew the pain of going back to bad times and remembering things you would rather forget.

121

"I was home watching TV when he was killed," she said. "It was all so stupid."

She stared at me for a moment and blew out a long breath before continuing.

"Our folks were in Seattle that week and I had their car. I told him to call me and I'd come pick him up. He said he would call if he was coming home, but he might spend the night at his friend's. When I didn't hear from him, I didn't think too much about it. He stayed over there sometimes. It wasn't a big deal."

"Where did he go?"

"Over to Devin's."

I thought back to the photo of Spenser's soccer team. I had looked carefully at the faces and names listed underneath to see if I recognized anybody. I didn't recall any Devin.

"Did Devin play soccer?" I asked.

Mo laughed for a second.

"No way. He wasn't, isn't that kind of kid. Spenser met Devin in school that year."

"So Spenser was walking home from Devin's house and then was hit by the car? I thought he was found out in the middle of nowhere, on a country road or something."

"Yeah. Devin lives out there. It's about three miles from us and Spenser liked to run it. That's what he did the night he died. He ran over to Devin's house, wouldn't let me take him. I don't know what they did all night. Normal stuff I guess. Probably video games or just listened to music for hours and then headed back home. Or tried to, until the bitch took him out."

She reached into her pocket and pulled out a package of cigarettes, taking one out and playing with it between her fingers. She was still composed, but she was on edge. I could tell she was done.

"I'm going to step out for a minute," she said.

I watched as she went out to the curb and lit a cigarette, the smoke striking against the black sky. I finished cleaning behind the counter and called Kate to let her know I was leaving soon. Mo came back in.

I grabbed my coat. We turned out most of the lights and stepped outside. She locked the door.

"So how do we do it?" she said. "How does he talk to me?"

"I don't really know. The ball's in his court. I'm sure he'll let us know."

She reached into her pocket and pulled out a pen.

"Hold out your arm. Here's your first taste of ink."

She wrote her phone number on my skin.

"Call me right when you see him. I'll come and find you."

# Chapter 25

I looked up at the sky. In the distance, black clouds clustered together and looked like they were coming our way. But we had some time.

I dribbled out toward the center circle, turned, and took it in. Ty was back in front of the goal.

He was a natural athlete. He biked, skied, rock climbed, and ran on trails. He did triathlons and had run a marathon.

But he sucked at soccer.

"Goooooaaaaalllllllll!" I shouted out as I threw up my arms and ran in circles around him. He laughed, retrieving the ball from the back of the net.

"I wasn't even ready yet. Go again."

The crowd in the next field cheered and I glanced over to see one of the teams celebrating. We were at Big Sky and a group of Hispanic men was playing nearby, their families watching on the sidelines.

I saw them out here sometimes. Over the last few months I had gotten to know a few of them, enough to say hi. They had even invited me to join in on their practices. I hadn't done it yet, but decided that the next time they asked I would play with them. They had some sweet skills, some with moves I had never seen before.

"Come on," Ty shouted behind me. "Bring it. Let's see what you got."

I scored on him three more times. Once, he literally ate my dust, as a made my best Iniesta move and he tripped over his own feet, falling down hard on the grass as he tried to stop me.

"Fogetaboutit," I said to him right before scoring. I took the ball out of the net as he got up, dusting off his butt.

I could hear one of players on the other field saying something in Spanish to one of his teammates.

*"Eres más malo que ese buey jugando contra aquella chamaca."*

"Go again. Now I'm really ready," Ty said, a little confidence leaving his body.

I smiled and gave him a thumbs up.

He wasn't really ready for me and he never would be. I knew that behind his gentle nature was a competitive beast. We could easily be out here all day, me scoring a thousand goals over and over again and him always getting the ball out of the goal and telling me to go once more. I liked that about him. I liked that a lot.

And I had to be honest. It felt good to be good at something. Especially something you loved.

I stopped counting my goals and then after a half hour or so, threw myself on the ground in the middle of the field and stared up at the sky. It was getting darker. Ty ran up and threw himself down next to me.

"Just an off day. Don't get a big head over it. Next time you're mine."

I laughed.

"Okay, I'll keep up on my practicing then."

He leaned over and kissed me.

"David says that I should be worried," I said, sitting up. It was a little bit of an embellishment, but that was the feeling I got after our chat at 10 Barrel. That Ty could start dating someone over there.

"About what?" he said.

"Well, that there are all these people you work with who you might want to go out with and that…"

"Take it easy, Abby. I'm not like that. You should know that by now."

I hugged the ball.

"I know," I said, trying to think of the right words. I was lost. "I guess I just wanted to say that I appreciate you being so…"

"Stop. I don't think you know what you're saying. You're fuzzy in the head right now."

"Well, I know we're taking it slow. I guess I wanted you to know that I have some really strong feelings for you."

He kissed me again.

"It's a special thing, this feeling. I've only been in love once, a long time ago. It's worth waiting for, Abby. Don't listen to your friend so much. I'm sure he's a nice guy, but he doesn't know me."

"Good to hear," I said.

We got up and headed to the parking lot, my heart ready to explode under my jersey.

And then I saw him.

In the trees, staring.

Waiting.

# Chapter 26

I turned to Ty.

"This is going to sound weird," I said. "But I have to go over there by myself for a few minutes. I've been having trouble sleeping and I read about this meditation technique. At this point I'm willing to try just about anything."

I knew it sounded lame, but it was the best I could do under the circumstances. I could tell he wasn't completely buying it. I bit my bottom lip. He looked at me for a minute, and then looked over at where I had pointed, then back at me.

"Well, I'll come along with you," he said and started heading in that direction.

I glanced over at Spenser, my chest tightening, and pulled Ty's arm.

"It's supposed to work better if you're alone. But I'll be right over there, in full sight, next to that tree. It'll just take a few minutes. I'll meet you at the truck."

He hesitated for a moment.

"Okay, whatever," he said, rubbing his chin. "But I'll wait right here."

"Thanks," I said.

I was hoping Spenser would stay longer this time. I needed more information and wanted him to tell me what really happened the night he died. I had a strong feeling that's why he was here. Maybe he just needed his family to know before he could move on.

As I walked up to him, the first thing I noticed was that he looked stronger, more like a teenager than a ghost. He wasn't so faded.

"Hi, Spenser," I said, trying to hide the horror I felt as I looked at his face. He was scary up close, the scar darker and thicker than before.

"Hey," he said, nodding.

He shoved his hands in his pockets and leaned against a tree.

"Is that your boyfriend?" he asked.

"Yeah," I said.

"He sucks."

"You were watching, huh?"

"Yeah," he said, grimacing.

"Hey, I talked to Mo about you the other night. She listened this time. I think she believes that I can see you. Do you want me to call her and let her know you're here?"

"No. I just want to talk to you. I want you to tell her."

"Okay."

I sat down on an old log and he sat next to me and we both looked out at the soccer fields. A family with small children was down by one of the goals, playing with a small ball.

"It was a bad night. The worst night of my life."

"Well, yeah. You died."

"Yeah. That too. But that wasn't the worst of it. Not even close."

I turned quickly and looked at him. His eyes were wide.

"Before you told me that you messed up," I said. "Tell me what happened. What did you do?"

He let out a ghostly sigh.

"It's what I didn't do. I should have listened."

"Listened to who?" I asked.

"My folks for one. My friends on the team. Even Mo told me."

"Mo told you what?"

But he didn't answer. He just stared out at the little boy who had picked up the ball and laughed as he ran toward us, his father chasing him.

"That he was bad news," he finally said. "But I just didn't see it. I thought he was okay. Different but fun. I was stupid, so stupid."

The junipers swayed in the wind.

"Are you talking about your friend Devin?"

"He's not my friend."

He stood up and started pacing in front of me.

"So what happened that night?"

"We were going to hang out, like we always did. His dad wasn't home. He worked nights. We usually just hung out and played music and video games. He had a drum set we goofed around with. Sometimes Devin drank beer and smoked pot."

"Not you?" I said.

"No. I was serious about my training. Always a big game coming up. I just sat and we talked about stuff."

"What kind of stuff?"

"Sometimes girls. Sometimes about teachers and kids at school we didn't like. He got in trouble a lot and was always getting sent off to detention. He was suspended once for setting a fire in the bathroom. Almost expelled, I think."

He was quiet for a moment, and I worried that he might start fading away, but he was just thinking.

"So you guys were just hanging out like that the night you died?"

"It started out that way. Then he says to me, 'McSorley, come with me for a minute. I want to show you something cool.'"

Another silence.

"So you went with him?"

He nodded.

"Yeah. I followed him outside. He lives on one of those ranches out in the country. You know, with lots of land around. There's this little shed behind the house, and Devin's walking to it. It's like dark as hell out there and I'm stumbling around like a zombie and wondering what's so important to interrupt our game of *Mass Effect* that he's gotta show me. And he opens the door to this little crappy shack and flips on some light and says, 'Welcome to *my* jungle' or some shit like that."

He sat down again and held his head in his hands.

"The smell was so bad. So bad. I could smell it before I even got to the door."

He looked up at me.

"It was sick. I wanted to puke right there, but he comes up to me and pulls at my shirt like really hard and makes me go inside."

I inhaled slowly, trying to shake the feeling that was building inside me. Spenser started touching his fingers together over and over as he watched the family running around on the grass.

"What was in there, Spenser?" I asked after a long silence. "What was in the shack?"

"Cats," he said finally. "Five, maybe more. All laid out on this long table. All without heads. Devin had decapitated them and nailed their heads up on the wall."

Chills ran up and down my back and I struggled to breathe.

"What did you do?"

"I think I screamed. No, I'm sure I did. And he just started laughing. He says to me that this was his sport. That he played games, too. Not soccer, but 'games.' And then he says he wants me to join him. And he pulls out a bag from the corner and I hear the meowing."

"Oh, my God," I said.

"He hands me the bag and tells me he wants me to do it. Slice off the head for the collection. It's the best feeling in the world he says. 'I want this for you, McSorley.'"

Spenser shook his head. He was crying. I didn't know what to say.

"I'm like, you're sick man. And he's laughing and I'm backing out of that shed and he's following me with the bag. And then he pulls out a knife. And he says that he'll just do it himself, that he'll show me how it's done."

I had seen my share of evil, but Spenser's story showed me that I wasn't finished learning.

"I didn't know what else to do. I grabbed the bag and ran. I ran as fast as I could across the field. I could hear him laughing behind me, but I knew he couldn't catch up. No way. But then I tripped. By the time I got up, he was on my ass. And he was crazy mad, calling me all these names and waving that knife around. I wasn't just scared for the cat I was holding anymore. I thought…"

He stopped mid-sentence.

"You thought he was going to kill you," I said.

Spenser looked over at me.

"No," he said. "I *knew* he was going to kill me."

He sat quiet for a moment and I waited. I didn't want to rush him. I knew that it took everything he had to be here, telling me his story. But I worried he would disappear before he had a chance to finish.

I cleared my throat and he started again.

"But something happened inside me. Even when I tripped and fell and I could hear him getting closer and closer, I decided that I wasn't going to let him have the cat. I was holding onto that bag with all my strength and I was going to fight to save it. I ran and ran in the dark, across the open field. I had no idea where I was anymore. Everything was so dark and still. All I knew was who was behind me."

I nodded.

"I ran right out onto that road. And that's when the car hit me. The next thing I know I'm mangled in some bush, and in a lot of pain. I taste blood in my mouth. And I can't move."

"That's terrible," I said, thinking the story was over. It wasn't.

"Devin found me. He found me and he walked up to me and saw that I was having trouble breathing. And then he takes out his cell phone and I'm thinking, good. Help is on the way. I'll be all right. I'm coughing up blood, but I can hold on. But no. The sick bastard isn't calling anyone. He's taking pictures. He's taking pictures of me. He says in a sweet, soft voice that he's always been curious about it. And then he asks me, Abby. He asks me how it feels to die."

"Oh, my God," I said. "My God."

I didn't have any words. None. My mind was sludge and I just sat there next to Spenser, wanting to scream or yell or hit something. It was beyond horror, this story he told me. I wasn't expecting it. I didn't want to hear it. I didn't have anything to comfort him with. I just stared out in front of me, seeing nothing, unable to speak or think or react.

Numb.

"I want you to tell Mo," he said. "Maybe it will help her to know."

"I will," I said. "I'll tell her."

"But Abby, that's not why I'm here. There's—"

A soccer ball suddenly flew between us and I jumped up and caught it in mid-air, throwing it back to the girl who was running in my direction. I knew before looking. Spenser McSorley was gone.

I stood up and stumbled in Ty's direction, feeling sick. Everything was spinning, Spenser's voice echoing in my head, the light leaving the world.

## Chapter 27

Ty put his arm around me as we walked back over to his truck.

"You're shaking, Abby," he said. "Are you okay? What happened over there?"

"I'm fine," I said, breathing in the cool air. "Really. Just give me one minute."

We walked in silence as he took off his jacket and put it around me. He pulled me close.

"You sure you're okay?"

I stopped and hugged him.

"I'm okay," I said. "Do you have any water?"

He opened the door.

"Yeah, sit down. I'll get it out of the back."

"You weren't really meditating back there, were you?" he said while I took a long drink.

"Ah, the hell with it," I said after a long pause. "I suppose this is as good a time as any. You're right, I wasn't meditating. There's something you don't know about me."

He smiled.

I tried to smile.

"Hit me," he said.

"I see ghosts."

I just put it out there. The smile left his lips.

"What?"

"You know. Ghosts. Dead people."

His light eyes looked like balloons being filled with helium.

"No way," he said. "You're kidding, right?"

I shook my head.

"There's a boy I keep seeing. He's the brother of someone I work with. He was over in those trees and I had to go talk to him."

I stared into his eyes, trying to read his mood. Ty was always the same. Not too much ever affected him. But this time he looked different, waves of dark energy dancing around him.

"I know it's a lot to take on," I said. "And I want to tell you more. But I can't right now. I have to get home. There's something I have to do."

"All right," was all he said, turning the key in the ignition.

We drove back to town in silence. The 20 minutes felt like 20 hours.

When he dropped me off and disappeared down the street, I stood there wondering if the truth was overrated, if I would see him again. If he would ever look at me the same. I wanted him to come back and hold me and tell me that it didn't matter. That he loved me anyway. That it didn't matter one bit to him that I walked in two worlds.

After I realized he wasn't coming back, I unlocked the door and went inside.

I took a shower, letting the water carry away my tears, and then I called Mo.

# Chapter 28

It was after three, but when she picked up it sounded like she was still in bed.

"Yeah," she said, making it sound like a salutation.

"Mo, it's Abby."

"I know," she said, followed by a long pause.

"Can you meet me?"

We agreed to meet at Thump. Mo said she needed caffeine but didn't want to deal with "the people I spend my life with." I headed downtown.

It was pretty quiet in the café. Only a few small groups of people were scattered at tables as soft jazz music played in the background. It felt a lot different than Back Street, but maybe that was just because I didn't work there.

I found a table in the back. Kate and I used to come here a lot. They had good coffee and I always liked the employees and as I sat there waiting, I realized how much I missed it.

It didn't take Mo long to show up. She flung the door open and got in line. I wasn't sure if she saw me, but after she got her drink she came straight over.

"Hey," she said.

She kept her sunglasses on. Her clothes were a little wrinkled. She sat down, gulping the coffee that must have been too hot to drink.

"Hey," I said.

"So what did he say?" she asked, taking off her glasses and throwing them down on the table. Her eyes had dark circles under them.

"He told me about that night," I said. "And some other things."

"Tell me," she said. "I'm ready."

## Chapter 29

After I told Mo everything Spenser had told me, she sat in a stupor, deep in thought or something more primal.

There wasn't much to do but sit there with her.

"I'm going to kill him," she said finally, controlled rage in her voice.

"No, Mo," I said. "That's not why I told you."

"He's dead already," she said, standing up.

I followed her outside and stopped her on the sidewalk.

"Mo, listen. Please. It's not like you can go over there and beat him up. He's not normal."

"This isn't your concern anymore. Thanks for what you did, but this is about my family. My brother. Devin killed him and he's going to pay."

We were standing in front of the Oxford Hotel and I was trying to keep my voice down, hoping she would do the same. There were a lot of people around.

"You're wrong, Mo. It is my concern. Spenser came to me. You can't just go over there and pummel Devin into the ground. We need to be smart about this."

"I can do what I want. And I'm not afraid of that little psycho. I told Spenser way back he was bad news. I saw it a million miles away, but he still was friends with him. Now, get out of my way."

"You've got to listen to what I'm saying. Devin isn't like us. I know what I'm talking about. I've dealt with this kind of thing before."

She pulled out a cigarette.

"Let's walk over to the park and talk for a few minutes," I said. "Please. Just give me five minutes."

She didn't say anything but took off toward the river and I followed, breathing the white stream of smoke that flowed behind her. We walked quickly, taking shortcuts across alleys and parking lots.

There was an empty bench not too far from the water. We sat down at opposite ends and stared at a large swan floating in the distance.

"Don't tell me I don't understand," she said. "I've dealt with plenty of freaks in my life. And I know how to put them in their place. I've never had a problem with that."

"I'm sure that's true. But I'm willing to bet you've never dealt with any murderers, have you? Real ones? Well, I have."

I hadn't planned on telling her about Nathaniel, but I did. I told her about what had happened to me on that island near the Canadian border, about the scientists who did experiments on me, and about Nathaniel trying to kill me so he could bring me back to life.

Mo's eyes grew wide when I told her the part about being strapped to a gurney and lowered down into a pool of water to drown.

"You can't go straight at him. As long as he doesn't know we know what really happened that night, we have the upper hand. But we lose that if he finds out. The brief satisfaction you'd get from hurting him won't be worth it. He's evil. Probably smart. We've got to be smart too. We need to think about this."

She sighed, a trace of reason returning to her eyes.

"Okay. So what do you suggest then?"

I sat back. I tried to think of a solution, something that would sound like justice being served. But I drew a blank. I had nothing.

"I don't know yet. I need some time to figure this out. All I know is that if you go over there now, you'll just tip him off that we know something. We don't want that."

She blew out a cloud in front of her.

"I can see that," she said, sucking down more smoke.

We watched as a group of goths went by. I saw her nod to one of them and he nodded back.

I didn't know what else to say to Mo. I was out of words. I wasn't even sure how we could convince the authorities that Devin was the one who was at least partially responsible for Spenser's death.

"I'll give you some time to think on it," she said. "I'll do the same."

She stood up and walked away, catching up with the group that had passed by. I sat there looking at the dark water.

# Chapter 30

We were on the sofa watching a show when I told Kate about Spenser. She muted the TV at first and then turned it off. By the time I had finished, she had a blanket wrapped around her shoulders.

"I don't even know what to say," she said. "It's too awful for words."

I just nodded.

Each of us alone with our thoughts, we sat quietly for a few minutes as the light left the sky outside. Then she got up and headed to the kitchen. I followed her.

"The granite is going to be nice," I said, running my fingers across the old, white tiles on the counter. We had lived in this house since we were kids and I remembered sliding little plastic race cars across them.

"Yeah, they're coming out next month," she said, opening up a cupboard. "You were the one who inspired me to order them, Abby. I thought that you might like to work in a really kicked-up kitchen."

"I didn't know that you were doing it for me," I said. "That was nice."

The kettle started whistling and she poured the boiling water over tea bags into two large mugs and handed me one.

"You know, back when you were up there on that island, I kept thinking that if I could just get you home everything would be okay."

I held the cup, letting the heat warm my hands.

"And then, when we were on the plane and I was looking out at the clouds at the pinks and blues of the sunset as we were landing, I thought about how there was nothing more important in the world than you making it back here. Nothing. And how lucky it was that I was sitting next to you, heading back to our little house."

I looked up at her, words stuck in my throat.

"I'm just so grateful that you are still here," she said, pulling out the barstool and sitting down next to me. "And every time I hear terrible stories like that, it chills me to the bone. But it reminds me again how lucky we are."

She tapped my arm with her hand and I patted her shoulder.

"Poor Spenser," she said, after a minute.

"So what can we do about it, I mean Mo and me?" I said after a while. "He can't just get away with it, Kate. But I've been racking my brain and I can't think of anything."

"You're right. It's tough. But it's not like you can drop by the police department and tell them that you know the real story about what happened to Spenser because you talked to his ghost."

"We need evidence," I said. "Evidence that proves that it wasn't just an accident."

Kate put her cup down.

"I think there's a good chance that Devin still has those photos he took of Spenser," she said. "Seems like he would want to hang on to something like that. I think he would consider it important, maybe a sort of trophy. But I don't know how you could get your hands on them. And even if you did, the pictures of Spenser dying won't prove anything other than that he's a sicko."

142

I nodded.

"Well, maybe the photos would be a good place to start," I said. "You really think he still has them?"

"The more I think about it, the surer I feel. Yeah, he still has them. I'm no expert but he really seems like a textbook case, don't you think?"

"What do you mean?"

"That he's a killer," she said, and I could almost hear the gears in her brain going around, faster and faster. "From what I know, these people don't have a normal childhood and then just freak out when they grow up. Most of the time there's a pattern that can be seen early on if people know what to look for. A lot of infamous serial killers started out torturing animals as children. Something draws them to that sort of thing. And then they get a taste for it. That's how it begins."

I shuddered.

"Begins?" I said.

"Begins," she repeated.

"Kate, we have to do something. We have to figure out a way so that people know that Devin murdered Spenser."

"Take it easy, Abby. First off, even if you were able to convince somebody that Devin chased Spenser out onto the road, that wouldn't qualify as murder. From what I've heard, you would probably have to show intent and that would be hard to prove. And also, remember that it was ruled an accident. And that woman did hit him while she was talking on the phone. In the eyes of the law, she was responsible for Spenser's death. So I don't know if you could really say that Devin *murdered* him."

"I suppose, but there's got to be something," I said. "You know, that woman might not have been able to stop in time even if she wasn't on the phone."

"I guess we'll never know. And I don't know if there is anything else you can do. Maybe Spenser just wanted to tell you his story so that his family could know. Maybe knowing what really happened that night will help them in a way, like with Annabelle Harrison's family."

"I already told Mo. But I don't think it helped. It only made her mad. She freaked out and was all ready to go over there and go off on him."

"She's not serious, is she?" Kate said.

"No, I talked her down. For now. But who knows how long it'll stick. She doesn't seem the type to ponder things to death. Sooner or later, she's going to take some sort of action."

Kate stood up and stretched and put our cups in the sink.

"I know you want to be able to help everybody solve everything, but I think your job is just to pass along the information. You did what Spenser wanted. You heard his story and told his sister. Try to move on."

I nodded.

"Come on," she said. "Let's watch Chef Ron to change the mood before we head to bed."

I did my best *Sweet Genius* impression and she laughed.

***

It was late when I turned on the computer and wrote to Claire.

I knew what Kate was saying was true, but it was hard to just let it go. I thought Claire might be able to shed some light.

Claire was a psychic who lived in London. I found her on the internet a while back when I was desperate and looking for Jesse. I wrote to her often and considered her a good friend, even though we lived so far apart and only communicated online.

I typed out some quick lines, updating her on the latest visit with Spenser along with a short summary of what had really happened to him. I was hoping she had an idea. I understood what Kate was saying about passing on information, but it just didn't feel like enough. Not in this case. There had to something more I could do.

I hit the send button and put the laptop back on my desk.

Exhausted, I got into bed and waited for sleep.

# Chapter 31

"Medium nonfat mocha double shot," David called to Mo, over my head.

I had been jittery all day and quickly ducked instinctually, a survival mechanism taking over, like his words would slam into my face and crack it open.

"Abby Craig, are you okay?" he asked.

I wasn't.

I had slept for an hour the night before. I was standing there taking orders and smiling at customers, but I felt off. Way off. My stomach ached and my head was pounding and I was dizzy.

"Rough night," I said to David, who was staring at me, waiting for an answer.

He raised an eyebrow.

"Rough in a good way or a bad way?"

I rolled my eyes, which made the pain in my head worse, and the woman at the counter smiled and handed me a ten dollar bill. I gave her change and David slipped behind me and made her drink.

"Why don't you take your break," he said. "Drink some coffee or something."

"Good idea," I said.

But Mike had other plans.

"Hey, Abby, would you mind making a delivery for me?"

"Sure," I said. I did these occasionally, usually to only a few special customers and some of Mike's family.

"I need to drop off our new African blend to a potential partner. I told him I would drop it by this morning, but I have some roasting to finish up."

I didn't mind. Getting out from behind the counter was just what I needed.

I went in the back, took off my apron, and grabbed my keys and wallet from the drawer. Mike walked me over to the door and handed me a large paper sack.

"Here's the address," he said. "It's not far. Call if you can't find it."

It was nice outside. I rolled down the window, the warm air in my face. I thought about being on the river, just below Big Eddy, floating the last stretch, the smells of early summer all around. Floating. Floating. Not so long now.

I crossed Portland Avenue and headed up 9th.

I hadn't been to Awbrey Butte in a long time. Dr. Mortimer's house was there. I missed him, a lot, and hoped he was figuring it out and on a road that would eventually lead him back to Bend.

I turned on Summit and then made a left. There was a long, steep driveway leading to a large house at the top of an overlook. I pulled in front of the garage, parked, grabbed the coffee, and rang the bell.

A tall man with a beard opened the door.

"Hi," I said. "Are you Steven?"

"Yes?"

"I'm Abby. Mike wanted me to drop off some coffee."

My voice was breaking in strange places, but not because I was nervous. I was just tired.

He took the bag and thanked me, but I noticed his face change suddenly as he looked over my right shoulder.

"Uh, oh," was all he said.

I turned around just in time to watch the Jeep roll down the driveway, and then down the embankment.

# Chapter 32

It wasn't the dumbest phone call I ever had to make, calling Kate and telling her I needed her help. But it was close.

"Sure," she said. "What's the problem?"

"Car trouble," I said. "Can you come get me?"

She hung up right after I gave her the address, not asking any more questions. I was glad and figured it was easier to explain in person. She arrived just a few minutes later in time to see the two men from the tow truck company tie down the Jeep with ropes and pull it up and out of the trees.

I had been watching from the sidewalk below. After Kate got out of the car, she slowly took off her sunglasses. Her mouth dropped open as she stood staring up in disbelief.

"Are you okay, Abby?" she said when she saw me.

"Yeah, I'm fine," I said. "I wasn't inside when it rolled down. I guess I forgot to put on the emergency brake. I'm not used to the hills up here."

"No kidding," she said. "Is there a lot of damage?"

"I don't know," I said slowly. "I hope not."

The Jeep had rolled backwards down the paved driveway for a little bit before veering off and tumbling down the dirt embankment. Thankfully it was stopped by a group of pine trees, otherwise it probably would have smashed to bits down on the street. Or crashed into a passing car. Or plowed into a house across the way. Or hit a pedestrian.

These thoughts floated around in my mind like balloons released into the air by a child. But I felt detached and far from them, not being able to connect any particular feeling to them.

Steve had called the tow truck and then brought me a soda while I waited on his front steps. I had put off calling Kate for as long as I could.

"What are you even doing here?" she asked.

I told her about the delivery.

"Let me go talk to them. You relax. Do you want to sit in the car?"

I nodded and she handed me her keys.

"Thanks," I said.

I watched as she walked up the driveway and talked to one of the men in a dark jumpsuit. I sat in the passenger's seat, not sure what day it was. *Jeepday. Oh, yeah.*

Kate came back in a few minutes and started the car. The men had put the Jeep on the back of their truck.

"I told them to take it to Midas, they do good work," she said. "And I stopped in and said goodbye to the owner of the house. Turns out I did a story once on him. He's part owner of a winery out here."

I wanted to go back to work, but Kate insisted on taking me home so I called Mike as we drove and told him I had delivered the coffee but was now having car trouble and wouldn't be finishing my shift.

When we walked into the house, I sat down on the sofa and stared at the blank TV screen. I was a little surprised I wasn't crying, but it seemed like too much of an effort. I didn't have the emotions or the energy. It wasn't a big deal anyway. Everything was okay. No one had been hurt. The Jeep would be fine. Everything. Would. Be. Fine.

"Besides the ding to the door, it doesn't look that bad," Kate said. "Of course there might be some damage we can't see. But I'll bet they can have it back to you in a day or two. You're lucky, Abby. It could have been bad."

"I know," I said, my voice small.

"I have to go back to work, but I'll be home early. You okay here by yourself?"

"Yeah, I think I'll just take a nap."

But I didn't get up and I didn't lie down. I just sat there looking at the TV.

"I want us to talk later," she said. "When I get back."

My mind wasn't working right, but I knew what she was going to say.

# Chapter 33

I was at the bottom of the lake again.

And like before, a train echoed loudly in my ears. My lungs burned. And then suddenly I was breathing in complete darkness. I struggled toward the familiar door, a faint glow escaping from the bottom. My feet moved in slow motion, sinking down into the cold ground.

The train kept roaring. I tried once more to push the door open, throwing all my weight into it. It gave way for a moment, moving a few inches before stopping.

I put my face up to the crack to look inside. There was someone there again, standing not too far away. He was dressed all in black and I gasped, remembering that Nathaniel was always dressed in black.

It felt like him, dark and troubled. My heart pounded, trying to match the train in volume, and I couldn't catch my breath.

I couldn't be sure. He wouldn't turn around.

"Nathaniel," I managed to croak. "Is that you?"

"Soon now," he whispered.

Just as he started to turn, a loud explosion ripped through the small room. Wild flames shot up toward the ceiling. He was dancing now, dancing in and out of the fire.

His face was in the shadows, but I knew that it was him. I ran back, ran back to the water, my forehead burning. Everything burning.

# Chapter 34

Ty dropped by just past seven, a six pack of beer in one hand and a bouquet of sunflowers in the other.

"For you," he said, handing me the flowers.

Kate was the one who called and invited him over for pizza and a movie. At first, I didn't want her to. I felt beyond foolish about the Jeep and there was, of course, that awkward silence the last time we were together right after I told him I saw ghosts.

But seeing him standing there, I couldn't help feeling glad he was here.

"Thanks," I said.

He kissed my cheek.

"You're kind of hot," he said, putting his hand on my other cheek.

"Nice of you to say."

But it was true. I wasn't feeling all that great since I woke up from my nap, right after I pulled myself away from seeing Nathaniel dance in the flames of that conflagration. I woke up in a pool of sweat. I downed a few aspirin, hoping that it would bring down the fever, but I guess it hadn't worked yet.

If Kate had noticed my flushed cheeks, she didn't say anything. And she pretended that she didn't hear Ty when he asked if I was okay.

"And these are for us," he said, handing the beer to Kate.

She was wearing her old sweats and had her hair up. She studied the bottles.

"What kind is this? I haven't seen it before."

"*Chainbreaker*," Ty said. "It just came out."

"*Chainbreaker*?" Kate repeated.

"Yeah, it's like an homage to cyclists."

"I'll open up a couple for us and put the rest in the box," she said.

After a slew of jokes about me getting some lessons on how to apply the emergency brake, we finally settled down into a conversation that didn't involve references to driver's ed. Ty told us about a celebrity coming into 10 Barrel that afternoon, which got Kate going on how she once interviewed an old cowboy actor who lived out in Sisters, a little town not too far away.

Then we talked about the Amphitheater's lineup for the summer. Kate was excited about seeing Norah Jones and Ty figured he'd probably go to all the concerts, listening to the acts he didn't feel like paying for from a boat out on the river. He liked being outside and loved live music and had already bought our Tenacious D tickets for the first show of the season.

After dinner, we saw one of the movies Ty brought over. It was something called *Driver*.

"Take notes, Abby," Ty said, smiling.

I rolled my eyes.

It was dark and odd and slow in parts, but it wasn't bad. Kate yawned through most of it and after it ended, told us she had to call it a night.

"No way," Ty said. "That's weak."

She smiled but left anyway.

"Okay, my turn," I said. "You know we haven't seen a classic in a while. I think it's time."

"If it can't be helped," he said, smiling.

I scrolled through the list of saved shows on the DVR.

It was something called *Far from the Madding Crowd*, starring Julie Christie.

"This is not a good sign," Ty mumbled as the overture began. He was probably still recovering from the elephant thing. "The orchestra playing before the opening credits is definitely not a good sign."

"Yeah, looks like it's a long one. We don't have to finish it tonight."

"And some people say there's no God."

It had been a good night, but I still could sense that little bit of space between us.

"So, thanks for those flowers," I said, looking at them on the table. "They're beautiful."

Ty put his hand on my thigh.

The movie began. It took a while to get going but after about an hour I could tell that Ty was even into it. There was a crazy part with a soldier pretending he was on horseback and a couple of wild scenes involving sheep.

"What's with you and animals?" he said.

I started laughing, and he joined in.

I paused the movie. I didn't know how to ask him, but I couldn't stand not talking about it either.

"What's up?" he said.

I glanced over at him and looked into his eyes and then checked his energy. It was still bright and buzzing quickly around him like a swarm of bees.

"I thought we should talk. You know, about what I told you the last time we were hanging out."

He pushed himself back into the soft leather.

"You mean the part about ghosts?"

"Yeah, that would be the part. I mean, were you surprised about what I said? Because it seemed like it freaked you out a little."

He nodded.

"Yeah. Sorry, but I was. I know all that stuff is really popular these days and everything, but I'm not into it. I have a lot of trouble taking it seriously."

I wasn't sure what that meant. Did it mean he thought I was lying? Or worse, did he think I was crazy? How could I be with someone who didn't believe in the things I saw, the things I knew were as real as the two of us sitting here?

I stared at the TV, frozen on the image of a coffin.

I could almost see how someone would find it funny, switching out my old boyfriend who is a ghost for a new boyfriend who didn't believe in them. It might have made for a good sitcom, but I was having trouble seeing the humor in it right now.

I sighed.

"I hope that's not going to be a problem, Abby," he said. "It's not a big deal. I'm crazy about you. It's not that I don't believe you. But it's just not my thing."

"All right," I said.

I didn't want to get into a big thing now. I was tired and my car had fallen off a hill and my mind was filled with thoughts of Spenser and Mo. I couldn't take this on right now.

"Let's talk about it later," I said, yawning into my hand. "And let's finish the movie next time."

"All right," he said. "Turned out to be a good one, in a squirrelly kind of way. I want to find out how it ends."

*Me too*, I thought. *I want to find out how this ends.*

\*\*\*

I heard a knock on my bedroom door. It was only closed over, but Kate waited until I asked her to come in.

"Ty leave?" she asked as she sat on the bed.

"About an hour ago. What are you still doing up?"

"Couldn't sleep," she said.

I put down the laptop. I had been checking my email, disappointed that Claire hadn't written back yet.

"Did you have a good night?" she asked.

"Yeah, I guess."

"You're not feeling bad about your Jeep, I hope. The insurance will pick up most of it. And sure, your premium will go up, but that's not important right now. Anyway, you can use my car if you want. Just drop me off at the paper."

"Thanks, Kate," I said, staring at my hands. "But doesn't a reporter need a car?"

"I'll use Tony's. Really. Please take it."

"Thanks," I said, counting my fingers.

"So what's the matter?"

I told her about Ty. Even though I had tried to put it out of my mind, I was struggling with it. In fact, it was making me angry.

"Maybe he's religious or something like that."

"That's what I was wondering," I said. "But I don't think that's it."

"He just needs more time to come around. You'll see."

"Maybe," I said. "But I don't get it. How can you have a relationship with someone you don't believe?"

"It's been my experience that relationships can work, or not work, for all sorts of reasons. They're always complicated and always seem to be hanging on by a heart string, or a thread. I think maybe the key is having enough common ground and spending time there."

"Thanks, Dr. Phil," I said. "But seriously, that all sounds true."

She smiled.

"I guess I'm still bummed about Barcelona," I said. "And it just keeps getting worse. First they lose the *Clásico* against Real Madrid. Then they get knocked out of the Champions League by Chelsea. And now I just read that Pep is quitting."

I knew Kate didn't know most of what I was talking about.

"Pep?" she repeated. "Isn't that that coach, the tall, dark, and handsome one?"

"Well, I don't know how tall he is, but, yeah, that's him."

"Gee, that's too bad," she said without much feeling. "He's a snazzy dresser."

I knew that some people, like Kate, might think I was overreacting. But when it came to soccer, there was no such thing. I couldn't sleep. My Jeep had rolled off a cliff. My relationship with Ty might be in real trouble. I was having visions of Nathaniel again. Spenser had been killed by his friend. All these things were true. But Barcelona had had a horrible week. That was true, too.

Kate walked to the window and looked out into the darkness.

"When are you starting on the backyard?" I asked.

"Next week. Those tulips I planted in the fall should be blooming soon. I'm going to do a Zen sort of thing back in the corner. Maybe a rock garden and a Buddha statue and a fountain."

"Sounds peaceful."

"It's going to be good," she said and then got to the point. "Abby, you need to listen to Dr. Krowe."

There it was. I knew it was coming but it was the last thing I wanted to deal with right now.

"At the risk of pointing out the obvious, what happened today with your car is a result of you not sleeping. And you

159

got off lucky. Very lucky. Next time or the time after that, things might not work out so well."

I stared at her.

"You have to sleep or you're going to really hurt yourself. You're going to have to trust me. Because you aren't seeing the entire picture right now."

"What's the entire picture?" I said.

She was quiet for a long time.

"That you're losing it," she said finally.

"You're exaggerating," I said.

I was staring up at my Messi poster wondering why he had missed that penalty kick. If he could have just made it, like he did most of the time, we would be celebrating Barcelona going on to the finals. I hated being angry with him, but that's how I felt.

I was starting to feel some resentment toward Kate as well.

"Sure, I'm a little tired, but nothing really bad has happened. I haven't had a breakdown. I don't spill hot coffee on myself or poison customers. I'm okay. The sleep thing is working itself out. Life is fine. I'm fine."

Kate folded her arms and shook her head. Dark waves rose off of her.

"Yeah, you're fine. Fit as a… Look, just take the pills, okay. Just for a week. Please, Abby, take those damn pills."

I didn't say anything. She waited and then shook her head again. Then she walked out, closing the door behind her.

I picked up the bottle from the nightstand and threw it against the poster.

# Chapter 35

In the morning I walked over to the park like I used to when I was a kid, bouncing the ball on the cracked side-walk and thinking about how everything felt so bad. I still felt hot and needed to get outside into the fresh air, clear my head.

And I needed to find Jesse.

The basketball court was empty. Today the whole park was empty. I scanned the outlying areas, seeing if anybody was lurking in the trees in the distance. But there was no one around.

I brought my basketball, the one I hardly ever used, the one buried in the back of my closet. I only kept it around because it reminded me of him, of the days when we would spend all our time at the park shooting hoops. By the time we were in high school though, Jesse insisted on always using his Michael Jordan ball when we played.

I took a shot, missing, and ran after it on the grass.

I needed his help. The vision of Nathaniel was still on my mind.

"Jesse," I whispered, taking another shot.

I couldn't remember the last time I called out to him. I was trying hard not to. I was trying hard to let him go. But he told me if I ever needed him he was there for me.

And I needed him now.

"Jesse," I called out again.

I took another shot. It hit the rim and from behind I heard a voice.

"Boink," he said.

I turned around and ran into his arms.

"Jesse," I said.

"Easy, Craigers," he said, tugging at his hat. "Let me show you how it's done."

We played for a few minutes, but not for long. The morning sun was in my eyes and shining down so bright that when Jesse ran into the light, he disappeared for a moment.

But he was still there, going up for a layup. He grabbed the ball and handed it to me.

"I'm glad you called," he said. "We need to talk."

His eyes sparkled with an urgency I didn't see too often.

We walked over to a cement picnic table and sat on top of it.

"Tell me what's going on," he said.

"Kate says I'm losing it and I think she may be right. Plus a few other things."

He studied me for a moment.

"She's right," he said, and then laughed.

"Come on." I elbowed him in the stomach.

"Okay, okay. Look, I know something's going on with you. And I know it's taking a toll. Your energy isn't the same. It's weaker or something. I had trouble finding you."

Icy fingers closed around my air passage.

"What do you mean? You can't see me anymore?"

He shook his head and put his arm around my shoulders.

"Step away from the edge, Craigers. No, it's not that. But your light is just different now, more diffused."

"So Kate is right?" I said.

"I don't know about that, but I've been trying to get with you to tell you. About that kid you're talking to. You need to—"

"I know," I said, cutting him off. "You want me to stay out of it. Leave it alone. Stop talking to ghosts."

"No, that's not what I was going to say. Actually, just the opposite."

I shivered in the cool wind.

"What? But you're always telling me to leave the ghosts alone and to get on with my life."

"I know, but not this time. You need to help him."

I couldn't believe it.

"Help him? You mean Spenser? I already did. I listened to his story and told his sister. But I'm afraid Kate's right. There's probably not much more I can do."

He stood up and picked up a pine cone, throwing it up and catching it.

"I can't see everything," he said. "I can't see most of it in fact. But something bad is coming. It's on the way, Craigers. And it's really bad. Black. Dark. And it has to do with Spenser."

I sat quiet for a moment, thinking.

"But it already happened to him, Jesse. He was killed."

He shook his head.

"That's not why he came to you. There's something more. You have to talk to him again and find out what it is."

I rubbed my shoulders, wishing I had brought my jacket. Wishing other things too.

"All right, I'll try to find him."

163

"Do it fast. Time is running out."

I shuddered again, remembering that Spenser had said the same thing to me when he was sitting at Back Street. The same exact words.

"Okay," I said. "I will. I'll try to find him today."

"Make it happen," Jesse said, his face serious.

I nodded. It was justice that Spenser probably needed, I was guessing. Somehow I had to prove that Devin was responsible for making him run out into the street.

"Okay, I have something else I need to talk to you about," I said. "It's not related to this, but I need your opinion."

He smiled.

"You need advice on your love life, don't you?"

I smiled awkwardly.

"Kidding," he said, taking my hand.

He still felt and looked and sounded just as real as when he was alive. Suddenly it all hit me, how much I still missed him. I squeezed his hand. He made me feel alive, like I didn't need sleep, like I could stay awake with him forever. Like this. Forever.

"What's going on?" he said.

"It's Nathaniel. I've seen him."

The words sucked the air out of my chest as I said them.

"Really?" he said, sitting back down next to me.

I told him about the visions I had being having, about the feelings connected to them, and about him dancing in the flames.

"He must be in Hell, Jesse. And I think he's reaching out to me, trying to find me, and pull me down there with him."

I said it with little emotion, but my eyes watered up as I looked off in the distance. It was the thing I feared most, the horror that kept me up at night.

"I mean it," I said. "I think he's coming back to get me."

Jesse got up and stood in front of me. Then he pulled me close, wrapping his arms around me.

"Craigers, it's not him. Nathaniel's not here. I know his energy and he isn't around you. I'm sure of it."

I pressed my face against his chest, praying he was right.

"How can you be so sure?"

"Well, I can't be one hundred percent sure. But I'm pretty sure."

"Really? But what about those visions I've been having?"

"Did you really see him? His face?"

I shook my head.

"Close your eyes for a minute and think about him," he said. "How he feels."

I did as Jesse asked, the darkness closing in all around me.

"Now release it. Think about the vision. Is it the same energy?"

A group of geese flew somewhere above us, honking. But I kept my eyes closed, thinking about the dark figure in the fire.

"I don't know. I want to say no, but it seems like it's him."

"That's your fear talking, getting in the way. I don't think it's him. But I'm not leaving you until I know you're safe, Craigers. Call me anytime you need me and I'll come."

I held him tight.

"But this other thing I'm talking about needs your immediate attention. It's important."

Then he smiled, kissed me, and walked away, fading slowly until there was nothing left.

# Chapter 36

Ty pulled up to Back Street and kept the engine running while I got out.

"Bye, Abby," he said.

"Thanks for the ride," I said, closing the door.

He looked kind of sad, but I couldn't think of anything to say to lighten the mood. That small silence between us wasn't so small anymore, but I couldn't spend time thinking about it right now. There was too much to do.

"Hey, I could swing by on my break and take you home after work," he said.

"That's all right," I said, talking through the crack of the open window. "I'm picking up the Jeep with Kate today. Thanks anyway."

"Okay, I'll call later."

I watched as he left, exhaust fumes trailing from the back of his truck and then went inside.

I appreciated that Mike and David didn't make any jokes about me forgetting to set the emergency brake. They both asked if I was okay, sounding sincere. Mike asked when I was getting my car back and David told me that he was glad I wasn't hurt.

"I don't think it's connected, but Steve signed on as a partner this morning," Mike said before he walked away into the back.

"Probably just doesn't want to get sued," David said, half joking.

"It was completely my fault," I said. "I was a space cadet yesterday."

"Just yesterday?" he said, that one eyebrow going up high again.

I was waiting for Mo to come in. We needed to talk and I wanted to ask if she had any ideas where I might find Spenser, like an old hangout or place he liked to go. She was scheduled to start at two. I was surprised to see Lyle walk through the door instead.

"Where's Mo?" I asked David.

"Sick," he said. "She called in right before you got here. I gave Mike the message."

"That's weird," I said.

"It's not *so* weird. She's been known to sleep one off now and then."

Still, I shivered at the thought that she might have gone over to Devin's house. The last time I had seen her she had been able to rein in her anger. But for how long? I knew it was just a matter of time.

"Damn it," I said, wishing I hadn't said that out loud. David looked at me.

"Why?" he asked. "You two girlfriends now?"

"No," I said, shaking my head. "Nothing like that. But we talked it out the other day. I just wanted to make sure we were still okay."

I helped a woman with long hair that reached down to her butt. She had been standing and reading the menu for five minutes, trying to figure out what to order.

I called Mo a few times during my shift but she didn't answer.

"Damn," I said under my breath this time. "Damn."

# Chapter 37

Kate picked me up at four and we went over to Midas.

I saw the Jeep sitting in the parking lot.

"We did a front end alignment on her and replaced a broken tail light," the man behind the counter said. "And you probably want to have those shocks replaced one of these days. You'll have to take it to a body shop to get the door fixed."

I paid the bill, handing over my credit card. The whole thing, including the tow truck, had cost just over $200. Not pretty, but it felt like I was getting off easy. It could have been a lot worse.

"Thanks," I said.

"Be careful out there."

It felt good to be sitting behind the wheel again.

"Pay attention this time," Kate said, reaching in and rapping her knuckles on the top of my head.

"I will."

I watched Kate drive off and got Mo's voicemail again. Then I headed toward China Hat Road.

# Chapter 38

China Hat was a long, two-lane road that shot out from the edge of Bend and wound through the Deschutes National Forest south of town. The houses were spread farther and farther apart as the ranches took over the landscape.

As I drove I couldn't stop thinking about how Jesse and Spenser had both said that I was running out of time. I worried now that they might have been talking about Mo. I didn't know what I was going to do when I got there. I just knew I had to look for her. I stepped on the gas, hoping she hadn't crossed some line from which there was no coming back, praying that I wasn't too late.

But I wasn't just looking for Mo. I needed to talk to Spenser again too. I thought that I might find him along the road where he died.

I didn't know exactly where that was or where I was going. But I had some clues to work with. I knew Mo lived somewhere near the Knott Landfill. I had heard her complaining once to David about how she could smell the trash when the wind blew the wrong way. I had been surprised she could smell anything with all the cigarettes she inhaled. I also remembered she had told me that Devin's house was about three miles away and that her family had put up a cross marking the spot where Spenser had been killed.

The sky was heavy with dark clouds and the promise of rain. The Jeep bounced hard over the railroad tracks. I remembered what the mechanic had said about replacing the shock absorbers. I kept my eye on the odometer, making sure not to go too far. The cross, if it was still there, should be coming up. Large drops began to beat down on the windshield.

I suddenly realized I didn't even know what type of car Mo drove. I didn't even know if she had a car. She had mentioned that she had her parent's car the night that Spenser died, but she hadn't said what it was. I supposed she could have even walked over, taking the same route her brother did.

"C'mon," I said, starting to lose hope. "C'mon."

I slowed down, thinking I had gone too far, when I saw the cross. I pulled over, parked, and got out, walking over and touching it.

The white paint was faded and his name was written vertically in black. There were a few old, dead flowers under it, crumbling in the rain.

"Spenser," I said. "I need to talk to you."

I looked around, but he wasn't there.

"Spenser."

Nothing.

The rain started falling in sheets.

I squinted, looking around at the fields around the marker. I could only see one house nearby. It had to be Devin's, I thought. But something was off. The cross, the spot where he had been killed, was on the wrong side of the house. If Spenser had been hit while he was heading back home, his body should have been found in the opposite direction, closer to town, not farther out toward the forest.

Of course it was all in line with what Spenser had told me. He had been running away from Devin, not even sure where he was going, not back home.

I wondered how the police had explained this, or if they had even noticed it. I would have to remember to ask Kate about it when I got back. It might be enough to reopen the case.

I stared back at the house again. It was rundown and almost looked abandoned. And then I saw it. The shed.

The little shack behind the house Spenser had talked about. The place where Devin played his sick games, cutting up cats and nailing their little heads up on a wall to display.

I started shaking uncontrollably in the pouring rain.

## Chapter 39

I wasn't sure what to do.

A faint whiff of smoke lingered in the air. I knew they were always burning things out in the country, but Mo flashed through my mind.

I had a bad feeling, a real bad feeling, that she was connected to this.

I left the Jeep by the cross and started walking, staying on the road. I stopped at the dirt driveway and studied the house, which wasn't so far from the street. Dark sheets and foil covered most of the windows. Paint was peeling off the wood and the railing on the porch was broken in parts.

It didn't look like anyone was around. There weren't any cars parked out front. And except for the sounds of the storm and an occasional passing car, it was quiet.

From where I was, I could get a better look at the shed. Or what was left of it. I could see now that it was a burned-out shell, broad, black marks staining the wood that remained standing.

Half of it was gone.

I thought about getting closer, but the evil coming off the place kept me away. It wasn't solid or liquid or gas, but was just as real, as if it had a chemical formula all its own like water or sulfur.

Suddenly my phone rang and I almost jumped back into the street. My hand was shaking so badly I could barely read the name on the screen.

"Mo?" I said.

"Yeah," she said.

"Are you okay?" I asked.

"What?" she said, the anger coming through in her voice.

"Never mind. What's up?"

"Seriously?" she said. "You called me like a thousand times today. What do *you* want?"

I laughed nervously.

"Oh, yeah. I... I just wanted to see if you need anything. David said you were sick."

I could hear her sigh loudly.

"I swear, the mouth on that guy. One day someone's going to show him what that hole is for," she said right before sneezing. "No, I don't *need* anything."

The line went dead.

I slid the phone back in my pocket. And then I saw the sheets moving behind one of the front windows.

I ran back to the Jeep, the skin on my arms alive with fear.

## Chapter 40

I got in and was about to start the engine when I saw him in the rearview mirror.

He was staring at me, those dark eyes looking even more troubled than the last time. There was an urgency in his expression that was building.

Water ran down my face as I tried to catch my breath.

"Spenser," I said.

Our eyes met again in the mirror.

"Did you see it? The shack? Did you see what he did?"

"I saw it," I said, confused. "Wait, you mean Devin did that? He burned it down?"

But he didn't answer, just grabbed his head with his hands.

"Spenser, I'm trying to figure out a way to prove that Devin is responsible for your—"

"NO!" he screamed, looking at me again. "Don't you understand? You're running out of time!"

My blood ran cold through my veins at the desperation in his voice.

"It doesn't matter what he did to me now. It's what he's going to do."

"Okay, but—" I said.

But before I could finish he faded away, those dark, worried eyes the last part of him to disappear into nothingness.

## Chapter 41

I drove home, hot and cold at the same time, thinking about Spenser and what he said. Understanding now.

Devin was planning something, something terrible, and somehow I had to stop him. But I had no idea what it was or how I could prevent it.

When I got home, Kate wasn't there. I found a note on the table. She was working late but would call later. Just as I finished reading it, my phone rang.

I picked up without seeing who it was.

"Abby, it's Dr. Krowe."

*Great*, I thought.

"Oh, hello."

"I wanted to see how you were doing," he said. "I don't make a habit of calling patients, but I wanted to make sure you were okay."

"I'm doing fine," I said.

"Oh, okay then. Good. How are those pills working out?"

I wasn't going to lie.

"I haven't taken any yet."

"So you're sleeping better now?"

"No."

He paused for a moment.

"I have some openings tomorrow. Do you want to come in?"

"Tomorrow?" I said. "I'm working."

"Well, I have a few openings at different times of the day."

I heard pages turning in the background.

"Let's see, I have an eight, a one, and a four o'clock."

I knew he meant well, but my sleeping problems were the least of my worries now. There were too many things going on and they were all starting to spin out of control, close to colliding and shattering to pieces.

I thought about Spenser telling me that the past didn't matter and that time was running out and about how Jesse had said the same thing. About Mo wanting to confront her brother's killer. I thought about that evil old house and how the sheets in the window had moved. I thought about Devin and what he might be planning.

And about how I couldn't put things together fast enough and how I didn't know if I could stop what was coming.

"Sorry," I finally said. "I can't. It's a busy time."

He cleared his throat.

"Well, you call me then when you're ready, Abby. I hope to hear from you soon."

We said goodbye and hung up.

I thought about Nathaniel and Devin and about how in some ways they were the same. Neither of them cared about other people. They took what they needed and left the rest, leaving behind broken lives. The image was strong in my mind of Devin taking pictures of Spenser while he lay there dying. It was the same thing. It was like Nathaniel and his research team taking those notes as they watched me drown.

On second thought, maybe Dr. Krowe could help me.

"I can come in tomorrow at one," I said, calling him back. "There's something important I have to talk to you about."

# Chapter 42

I talked to Kate when she finally got home. It almost felt like old times, her working these long hours. I told her what Spenser had said, but not about going over to Devin's house.

"I don't know what he's up to, what he's planning," I said.

"I suppose it wouldn't do any good to confront him," she said. "It would be dangerous too."

"No, I don't think we want him to know we're on to him. But on the other hand... I don't know, maybe he would stop if he knew he was being watched. Oh, I'm seeing Dr. Krowe tomorrow. I think I'll ask him what he thinks I should do."

"Good," she said. "That's a good idea."

The rain wasn't letting up. I crawled into bed with my computer and checked my mail. Someone wrote asking if I had signed up for the summer soccer league yet. David invited me out for another beer, claiming I still owed him. I saved Claire for last.

*Hi Abby,*

*I would agree that helping this spirit is a good idea. I can't see him, sorry to say, so I can't offer any particular*

*advice. Do what you can, but keep in mind that sometimes
we can't always help them in the way they would want us
to.*

*Just do your best.*
*Cheers,*
*Claire*

I turned out the light, leaving Florence+ the Machine
on low, sleep carrying me down.

\*\*\*

I swam through the darkness, pushing my arms through
the black, heavy water until I got to the other side, the side
where I could walk and breathe again.

I staggered through shadows, the light somewhere
up ahead, coming from the door. My hand trembled as I
pushed on it. To my surprise, it opened easily this time. I
was able to walk inside. Finally.

He stood at the far end of the room, looking in a mirror, music pounding loudly against the walls. Guitars, like
weapons of mass destruction, raining down.

*Hell-black night has come today...*

He was dressed in black and again had his back to me,
screeching along with the song.

*In the moon your blood looks gray...*

He walked over to a mirror and stared at his reflection, running his fingers down over his hair. He whispered
something I couldn't hear. I moved closer, trying to get a
look at his face. He pulled his hood over his head, a few
strands of hair falling down on his forehead, the sweatshirt
tight over his bulky chest.

As he pulled on his belt, he turned suddenly. I jerked back. He was standing right in front of me. My heart
pounded like the drummer in the song. I saw his face, the
coldness in his dead eyes.

180

I was right there in front of him, but he didn't see me. Devin didn't see me.

He danced back over to the mirror, singing.

*Welcome to your death ballet...*

The train rumbled by again, blowing its whistle.

When the song ended, he went over to the desk, to a black box with wires and a clock attached. I watched as he set the clock to 9:15, the digital numbers lighting up brightly in the room. Then he placed it carefully in his backpack and zipped it up.

He smiled and whispered again, but this time I heard the words.

"Today you die," he said. *"Today you all die."*

# Chapter 43

I called Mo on my way out, relieved that she picked up after the first ring.

"Which high school does Devin go to?" I said, a high-pitched shakiness in my voice.

It was 7:55. There wasn't much time.

"Abby?" she said, sounding distracted.

"He's got a bomb, Mo," I said. "And he's going to use it today. Which high school?"

"I… I guess Bend High," she said. "That's where Spenser was supposed to go. Hey, how do you know all this?"

"Thanks," I said.

"Wait," she said as I started to hang up. "I want in."

"Where are you?" I asked, hitting the garage door opener and jumping in the Jeep.

"At work. I opened this morning."

"All right, it's on the way. I'll be there in five minutes. Be waiting outside. We don't have much time."

"I'll be ready," she said.

\*\*\*

After Mo got in the car, I stepped down hard on the gas and raced down Franklin. I threw her my phone and told her to hit number two and put it on speaker.

"Kate. He's going to blow up the school," I shouted. "Bend High. Devin's got a bomb. I saw it in a vision."

"Wait, what Abby? Calm down. Tell me where you are."

A car honked at us as I swerved around him, cutting back in his lane.

"He's at Bend High. Mo's with me. I saw it, Kate. The bomb. The time. Devin. It's going off at 9:15."

I glanced down at the clock on the stereo. There was just over an hour left.

"Okay," Kate said. "I'll make some calls. In the meantime, don't do anything stupid."

"Thanks."

I crossed 3rd as the stoplight went from light to dark.

"So you have visions, too?" Mo said. "In addition to seeing ghosts."

"Yeah, I've got more gifts than Santa Claus," I said.

I turned right on 6th. Groups of kids were walking lazily toward the school on both sides of the street. I forced myself to slow down.

The visitor parking lot was full, so I left the Jeep in the bus lane in front of the school. An incensed bus driver waved his arms and yelled at me as we ran up the steps to the office building.

"We need to talk to the principal now," I said to a woman behind the counter. The front office was full of students.

"Do you have an appointment?" the woman said, her voice heavy with smugness. "You need to make an appointment."

"Now!" Mo screamed. "It's a fu— It's an emergency."

A look of terror passed over her face.

"There's a bomb in the building," I whispered.

She picked up the phone and a few moments later we were escorted back to a conference room.

The man at the table motioned us to sit down.

"Yes," he said into the phone. "That's right. We are evacuating the school. This is *not* a drill."

"I'm Principal Mulwray," he said, looking at me after he hung up. "You must be Abby."

"Yes, but how—"

"Your sister just called," he said as piercing bells starting going off. "She told me you have some information about a bomb?"

"Yes," I said. "One of your students has brought a bomb to school today and it's set to go off at 9:15."

I didn't know how I was going to explain how I knew all this, but he didn't ask. He started typing something in a computer.

"Do you know his name?" he said. "This student."

"Devin," Mo said. "Devin Cypher."

He looked up, shaking his head and swinging the screen toward us so we could see his picture.

It was the same face I had seen in the vision. Same hair, same dead eyes.

Devin.

"Yes, that's him," Mo said.

"That's good and bad," he said. "He's not here."

He picked up the phone again and punched in some numbers.

"What do you mean?" I asked.

He held up his hand.

"Hello, Linda," he said. "You might have a serious problem over there. I just learned that one of your students, a Devin Cypher, might have a bomb on him. Yes, that's right. Supposedly he's planning to set it off at 9:15. Okay."

"He used to go here," Mr. Mulwray said to us. "But now attends the new high school, Desert Wind. Almost a third of our students made the move this year, including Devin Cypher."

"Damn it," I said to Mo. "We're in the wrong place."

We passed two security guards as we ran toward the Jeep. Several classes were already outside.

The alarms kept sounding.

# Chapter 44

*8:39*

Jesse was right. It hadn't been Nathaniel in my visions. It had been Devin all along.

I thought about this as we sped over to Desert Wind, Mo giving me directions.

And I was there. I was watching Devin the whole time, not realizing it. As the years went by, he had descended deeper into evil, from torturing helpless animals to being responsible for Spenser's death to *this*.

"Right here," Mo yelled.

I hit the brakes, the tires squealing as I took a wide turn.

"Then left up there at the stop sign."

There was a lot of commotion when we pulled up. Sirens wailed from all directions and mixed in with the alarms coming from the school. Students were being led in the direction of the football field, away from the buildings. Several classes were already there. School buses were lining up in front of the stadium.

The teachers did their best to keep order, but just as I remembered when I was back in school doing fire drills, it was hard for students to take it seriously. Practicing these things was important, but it also couldn't help resulting in a *boy who cried wolf* kind of reaction.

*It's real this time*, I thought. *He's here. The wolf is here.*

8:47

Police were pouring into the school.

I gripped the steering wheel to keep my hands from shaking as we sat in the Jeep across the street, watching as some of the loaded buses began leaving.

"Where do you think they're going?" I said.

"I don't know," Mo said. "I guess they want to get them as far away as possible."

I wondered where he was. Where the bomb was.

"Where do you think he is?" Mo said.

"I was just asking myself the same thing. I don't know. Maybe he took off."

A car pulled up behind us. It was Kate.

"Have you seen a photographer?" she said, walking up.

"No," I said.

"I can't believe that guy. He should be here. He left 10 minutes before me."

"Kate, this is Mo," I said.

"Hi, Mo," she said. "I can't tell you how sorry I am about your brother."

Mo nodded.

A small crowd had gathering by the parking lot. The police began blocking off the perimeter of the school. Kate tried to get through, but she was turned away. She interviewed a few bystanders and came back to where we were.

*8:58*

We stood in the weak sunlight, listening on Kate's police scanner.

"All clear," we heard. "All civilians have been evacuated. Repeat: all clear."

*9:03*

The street was jammed with cars, mostly parents coming to pick up their children. They were being directed to go to the parking lot by the football stadium.

"The device has been found," a voice said on the scanner. "Bomb Disposal Team report to the gymnasium. BDT to the northwest end of the gym."

"Roger that."

I looked at my watch.

"Hurry," I mouthed. "Hurry."

*9:08*

The seconds ticked by, simultaneously in slow motion and at the speed of light. An eerie hush fell about the place. Kate shook her head.

"How can this be happening?" she said.

"I'm surprised it doesn't happen more often," Mo said, blowing a ring of smoke into the air. "There are a lot of broken, messed up freaks walking around out there. Busloads of 'em."

*9:13*

I braced myself for what was coming, not wanting to look in the direction of the building.

"Device has been neutralized," we suddenly heard a moment later. "Repeat: device has been neutralized."

I closed my eyes and inhaled deeply. It felt like my first breath of the entire morning.

Kate reached out and squeezed my hand.

"You did it, Abby," she said.

"I had some help," I said slowly, looking at her and Mo and thinking of Spenser.

*9:21*

"Suspect's name is Devin Cypher. Whereabouts unknown. Suspect considered armed and dangerous. Proceed with extreme caution."

It was only a matter of time now before they caught him.

*9:28*

"Suspect is on one of the school buses. He may have hostages!" we heard a voice shout from the scanner. "Bus Number 9243. In the stadium parking lot. Bus Number 9243. All available units report to the stadium parking—"

Suddenly a loud, sickening explosion came from that direction. Flames and smoke rose in the air.

People were screaming.

# Chapter 45

Devin had boarded one of the buses and was sitting in the back. One of the other students came up and told the teacher he thought Devin might have a weapon. Mr. Collins, my old history teacher from Bend High, then told the bus driver to make an announcement, saying that the bus was having mechanical problems and that students would need to start getting off.

What happened next is unclear, but apparently at some point someone shouted, "My God, he's got a bomb!"

"All hell broke loose," one of the students later said during an interview. "Everyone started pushing and running."

Everyone except Mr. Collins.

According to the bus driver and several students, Mr. Collins went toward the back of the bus, where Devin was sitting. No one knows what he was thinking. Maybe he was trying to keep Devin away from the other students and give them enough time to get off the bus. Maybe he was trying to talk Devin down.

All that we know for sure is that a minute later the bomb strapped around Devin Cypher's chest went off, killing him and Mr. Collins.

## Chapter 46

I found my black skirt in the back of the closet, went into the bathroom, and slipped it on.

"Not used to seeing you in a dress, Craigers," Jesse said.

I sighed.

"It's a skirt. And if I never have to wear one of these stupid things again in my life, that'd be okay," I said, pulling it around in circles on my waist after I realized it was on backwards.

He was sitting on my bed, playing with my iPod as I got ready for the funeral.

"It's nice you're going," he said, not looking up.

I hated funerals. I hated everything about them. The smell of the incense hanging in the air, the way the light looked as it filtered through those stained glass windows. The shiny casket up front. All those tears and swollen faces.

But mostly I hated that somber, dark feeling that lodged deep down between the ribs when everything was over, that feeling that stayed around for a long, long time.

"He was a good guy," I said. "And a cool teacher. One of the few I ever had."

"Yeah," Jesse said.

I clipped my hair back and closed the closet door.

"I just wish I could have…" I said.

"You saved hundreds of people," he said. "I know it's hard to remember that now, but you will someday."

I wiped at my eyes and Kate called from the living room.

"Almost ready, Abby? We have to get going if we want to get seats. It's going to be packed."

"One minute," I yelled back.

I grabbed my black cardigan off the chair and put it on.

"Hey, by the way, you never went to mine," Jesse said, standing up.

"I would have loved to have gone to your funeral but I was in the hospital recovering, remember? You should know, you were there with me."

"No," he said. "I mean my grave. You still haven't gone to my grave, Craigers."

"No," I said. "Not yet."

"Well, maybe it's time," he said.

I grabbed my phone.

"See you later, Jesse," I said, squeezing my arms tight around him.

***

I was glad that Kate had made us get there early so we could get a seat. We sat in the back, but with an hour to go before the services, every seat in the church had been taken and there was a large crowd standing behind us.

The pews were filled with some of the people I had gone to school with. I talked to a few of my old soccer teammates, said hello to some teachers, and nodded at Conner sitting a few rows up.

192

The administrators at Desert Wind had closed the school for the day in remembrance of Mr. Collins and to allow students and faculty to attend his funeral. But because they were expecting so many people, cameras were set up and the service was broadcast back at the school.

As I sat listening to the priest, my mind began to wander over the events of the last few days.

I couldn't stop thinking about Devin. It came out in the newspaper articles that he had been in trouble a lot. His father refused to talk to reporters when they asked him why Devin did it.

During a search of Devin's room, police found something strange. It was mentioned in one of the stories in *The Bugler* and later picked up by the local TV stations. Devin had a series of photos of an injured boy who was bleeding from the head. Officials weren't releasing his name.

When investigators got around to asking me how I knew what Devin was planning, I just came out with it.

"I had a dream," I said.

They seemed skeptical. I didn't care.

Dr. Krowe had been able to see me the day after the bombing. I had asked him about evil. Because I couldn't figure it out, couldn't get a hold on it. Were people just born that way, like babies with a birth defect, or did it have to do with how they were raised? In many ways Nathaniel and Devin couldn't have been more opposite, yet they were both killers.

"I don't know, Abby," Dr. Krowe said, placing his glasses up on top of his balding head. "I've dealt with a lot of Devins over the years, too many, and I still couldn't tell you why they do it."

I nodded, appreciating the honesty.

"But maybe it's not your job to try and figure them out," he said. "Maybe it's about you staying one step ahead of them, like you did with those kids."

The priest finished his prayer and the eulogies began. There were a lot of tears.

When it was over, the priest walked down the stairs swinging the thurible from a chain, white smoke rising up and around the casket as he circled it in prayer. Soft sobbing echoed off the walls as the procession began and Mrs. Collins and their three young children followed the coffin down the aisle out into the glaring sun, never once looking up at the crowd.

I remembered what Pep Guardiola had said when Chelsea eliminated Barcelona.

"Sometimes you smile, sometimes you lose."

Today we all lost. And there were no smiles.

## Chapter 47

Breakups are hard. Tough. But sometimes, there isn't a choice.

We walked along the river until we got to the Big Eddy rapid and then sat on some rocks near the white foam cascading down in front of us. Mist floated upwards, touching our faces. We were quiet.

It had been a long hour and I was tired of talking. And even though our relationship was about to crash on the rocks, I still felt good about telling Ty everything. I was tired of keeping secrets from him. If he couldn't handle it, that was another story. I wasn't going to hide anymore.

And I couldn't just keep ducking from his calls or leaving messages saying that I needed more time. We would be guiding together in a few weeks and seeing each other on the river most days. We had to figure it out, end it amicably.

Ty knew all the details of the bombing like most everyone in Bend. Probably like most people in the country. And he knew from Kate that I was involved somehow, although he didn't know the specifics.

So as we walked on the trail that followed the river up to the rapids, I filled him in. Leaving nothing out.

"I didn't ask for this," I said, after talking about the visions of Devin. "None of it. Everything changed when I drowned in that lake. Everything. This is something that found *me*. And now it's who I am."

I watched his gentle white energy turn a little darker as the story about Devin progressed. I could tell he wanted to ask a question, but he didn't. He just listened.

But we had been sitting for a while now, the story done, and he still hadn't said anything. I stared at the whitewater and told myself to be strong.

I looked at my watch.

"I've got to get going soon," I said. "Shift starts at two."

I was hoping David was working today. He seemed like a perfect friend to talk to about this kind of thing.

"Abby," Ty said finally. "First off, I'm so sorry you had to go through all that."

He moved to a closer rock and took my hand. But it didn't make me feel any better. I had already made a decision. I couldn't be with someone who didn't believe me. It wasn't going to work out.

"Yeah," I said.

We sat for a moment watching an early season kayaker dressed in a wet suit, walk up to the river and study the rapids, his hand out over his eyes blocking the sun. It was unusual for them to go down solo. It was a permit-only section and mostly the rafting companies took people down.

"Going down?" Ty asked, his arms resting on his knees. He already had a nice tan going.

"Yeah," the guy said. "I'm looking to avoid that nasty pocket over there."

"Good idea," Ty said.

I smiled. We always tried to avoid the nasty pocket, too.

When he left, Ty looked back over to me, reaching toward my face. He lifted up my sunglasses and put them on top of my head. He did the same with his and moved even closer.

"I know I hurt your feelings that day at the park," he said. "And I'm sorry about that. But you're not the only one, Abby, that has things in their past that they're dealing with. And everybody deals with them different."

I nodded.

"Now, that was a terrible, terrible thing you went through last week. All I can say is that I wish you would have let me in. Let me help you in some way."

"And that's the exact reason we can't be together, Ty. I don't think I could have asked you for help. Not when you think I'm crazy."

He sank back, looking sad.

"I'll take responsibility for that day," he said. "I shouldn't have left it like that. That's my fault."

I didn't say anything. I wasn't sure if it was his fault or not. It was how he felt.

"But I don't want to lose you, Abby. I'm falling in love with you. I am in love with you." He looked away quickly. "And I've been waiting for this for a while now. This feeling. I don't want this to end. Just tell me what to do and I'll do it."

His words were nice, filling my heart, but I still couldn't see a way around it.

"I can't tell you to believe me when you don't," I said. "And I don't want you pretending. I'll know if you're lying."

"But can't you give me a little while? Why can't you be a little more flexible? More understanding."

I sighed. He was twisting everything up.

"I need to be able to talk about these things if I'm with you," I said. "And I need to know you don't think I'm crazy.

And I don't want to have to prove anything. I don't care about that anymore. I'm not out to convince people. They believe me or they don't. But the person I'm with has to, Ty. And you don't. I don't see a way around that."

He inhaled slowly.

"Is it because of your religion?" I asked.

"Religion?" he said. "My religion is the sky and the river and the trees. You know that."

I looked over at him as he tried to think of more words to say. His energy was lighter again, swirling around in quick circles. As I stared at him, that fluttery feeling bubbled around inside.

"Abby, I don't think you're crazy or lying or anything like that. I promise you. You saved all those kids at the school and that was amazing. And I totally believe that some sort of supernatural something happened."

He stopped for a moment, choosing his words carefully.

"Can't you just understand that I'm not comfortable with it? Why does that mean we have to break up?"

We were quiet for another minute and watched as the kayaker squeezed into his boat and paddled out to the calm stretch of the river, before turning into the roar. He sailed down the rapids, avoiding the whirlpool, like he had done the run a hundred times.

Ty stood up, offered me his hand.

"Come on," he said, smiling. "I don't want you to be late on my account."

I took his hand, and as he pulled me up I smiled at those crazy feelings surging through me again. It was nice, having feelings like this.

"Maybe we can try," I said, squinting in the sun.

Ty came closer and gave me a long, long hug.

## Chapter 48

It was those large, empty holes that always chilled me the most in cemeteries. The ones freshly dug out and waiting, the holes that would forever swallow the dead.

We strolled past one, a shovel thrown next to it on the grass, and I shivered.

"Damn," I said, smoke floating up into my face. "I hate those."

Mo took another hit.

"I'll meet you," she said and took off down the narrow cement path that led past rows of tombstones.

I didn't follow. I knew she wanted to be alone. I could visit Spenser's grave later.

She had wanted to come with me when she found out I was stopping by the cemetery after work. I was surprised, but glad for the company, even if she didn't say too much. It was a cold, gray day, but the rain had stopped and the clouds were breaking up above.

I walked toward the east, past three angel statues and an enormous Celtic cross.

It had been a few weeks since the bombing and I was still trying to get my head right. But it was getting better. Lately I thought about all those kids we had saved. They had been in the crosshairs of a killer and hadn't even known it. And it was a good feeling knowing that they were all still alive, thinking about tests and soccer and homework and football games and friends and kissing and the coming summer. They all had their lives out in front of them and it felt good that I had helped.

As I walked through the cemetery, past all the gravestones and flat markers in the grass, I smelled the bouquet of flowers I was holding in my hand. I had brought a mix of roses and daisies and irises, and kept the flowers close to my face so they would hide the tears in case he was around, watching me.

I knew where he was buried. And he was right in mentioning it. There was a reason I hadn't come before.

But I was ready now.

When I walked up, I shivered again.

Then I placed the flowers on the grave, said a soft prayer, gliding my fingers over the stone.

Over Jesse's name.

*THE END*

The adventure continues…

## *44 Book Five*

Now available

## ABOUT THE AUTHOR

Like her main character, Jools Sinclair lives in Bend, Oregon. She is currently working on *44 Book Six* as well as the first volume of a new series.

Learn more about Jools Sinclair
and the *44* series at…

**JoolsSinclair44.blogspot.com**

Made in the USA
Las Vegas, NV
26 November 2022